A
Harlequin
Romance

OTHER
Harlequin Romances

by REBECCA STRATTON

1748—THE GOLDEN MADONNA
1770—FAIRWINDS
1799—THE BRIDE OF ROMANO
1816—CASTLES IN SPAIN
1839—RUN FROM THE WIND
1858—ISLAND OF DARKNESS
1883—AUTUMN CONCERTO
1898—FIREBIRD
1913—THE FLIGHT OF THE HAWK
1942—THE FIRE AND THE FURY
1955—MOON TIDE

Many of these titles are available at your local bookseller,
or through the Harlequin Reader Service.

For a free catalogue listing all available Harlequin Romances,
send your name and address to:

HARLEQUIN READER SERVICE,
M.P.O. Box 707, Niagara Falls, N.Y. 14302
Canadian address: Stratford, Ontario, Canada N5A 6W4

or use order coupon at back of books.

PROUD STRANGER

by

REBECCA STRATTON

Harlequin Books

TORONTO • LONDON • NEW YORK • AMSTERDAM • SYDNEY • WINNIPEG

Original hardcover edition published in 1976
by Mills & Boon Limited

ISBN 0-373-02006-6

Harlequin edition published September, 1976

CHAPTER ONE

BEING in Italy gave Rosalind the feeling of being an entirely different person, and it was not only the blue skies and the sunshine, but something to do with the nature of the country itself and with the Italians. Rosalind had been in Italy for just over a week now, and in a small place like Crisdorfi it was not difficult to make friends, especially with the cheerful, olive-skinned and dark-eyed people who inhabited the beautiful Amalfi coast.

Crisdorfi was if anything even prettier than most of the small places that were spread along this coast, dotted at intervals among the volcanic cliffs. Like them Crisdorfi's varied crops flourished on an escalation of neat terraces that had been gouged from the rock and staggered down the cliff face like a colourful patchwork of citrus trees and sweet almonds, apples, pears and tomatoes.

Dark volcanic sands lapped by the warm waters of the Mediterranean made a foreground for the tiny quay, the cream-coloured houses and the fertile terraces above, the whole scene looking as if it had been painted against a backcloth of blue skies.

The people of Crisdorfi were industrious, necessarily so, for the maintenance of the terraces and their crops depended upon it, but they were unfailingly cheerful and friendly too and Rosalind found them just as delightful as their environment. In fact it was all so perfect and picturesque that sometimes she had to remind herself that it was real and not just the figment of some design artist's imagination.

Very few tourists found their way to Crisdorfi, although they might catch a glimpse of it as they passed along the Amalfi motorway in their coaches. No one ever stopped, for the steep, narrow road through the village down the face of the cliffs was enough to deter all but the most determined of explorers.

Being the only stranger among the native Italians brought Rosalind more than her share of interest, apart from the fact that she was a very attractive girl. Her bright, fair hair drew more than casual glances from the black-eyed young men of Crisdorfi, and they expressed their appreciation with rolling eyes and white smiles that beamed across their dark faces with unmistakable meaning.

Rosalind was more slender than most of the local girls, but the young men were no less impressed, for although she was slender, her figure was softly rounded and unmistakably feminine. Her eyes were a deep blue that sometimes looked almost violet in the shadow of thick brown lashes and she never wore a hat so that her blonde hair shone silkily in the bright sun, flattering the light tan she had managed to acquire during her first week.

She was returning from a shopping expedition in nearby Bellaporto and, as she made her way down the steep, winding road from the motorway, she inhaled appreciatively the scent of the lemon trees that was everywhere in Crisdorfi, and even sweetened her room at the Villa Gardina.

From the road as it wound steeply downwards, the view was spectacular. The little bay, wedged snugly into the lush green coast, was a deep, bright blue and the small anchovy fleet seemed no more than a child's game with toy boats bobbing on the turning tide as it licked at the honey-yellow stone quay.

From somewhere close by a child wailed indignantly, inconsolable even by the fluid stream of comforting words in a woman's voice, while a man sang to himself, happy with his lot. It was, Rosalind decided, almost too good to be true, and she would be sorry when her two weeks' holiday was finished and she had to go back home.

The Villa Gardina, where she was staying with Signora Vincente, was one of several perched at various points among the cultivated terraces on the cliff face. It was built about half way down, surrounded by its small but pretty gardens and with a breathtaking view of the bay, and Rosalind could still scarcely believe her luck in being there.

In fact it was purely by chance that she had heard of it. Some friends had spent a motoring holiday in Italy last year and Signora Vincente had let them have the use of a room for the night when they were unable to find hotel accommodation. With a little persuasion they had induced the Signora to let the one night become three, for they had found Crisdorfi so fascinating and attractive that they were reluctant to leave, and they had unhesitatingly recommended it to Rosalind when she mentioned taking her holiday in Italy.

Normally the Signora did not accommodate visitors, but when Rosalind wrote and explained that her friends had recommended not only the village but also the hospitality of Signora Vincente, she had agreed to make an exception for two weeks, and so far neither Rosalind nor her hostess had had reason to regret the decision.

Signora Vincente was an excellent cook and Rosalind ate well, her room was comfortable and there was no language problem either, for the Signora liked to practise her English whenever she had the opportunity.

Her room gave a breathtaking view of the bay across the tops of orange and lemon trees that wafted their heady scent towards her on the light wind blowing in off the sea. A perfume that was supplemented by the mass of roses that Signora Vincente grew in her garden along with geraniums and carnations.

There were several other houses, some smaller and some bigger than the Villa Gardina, but they were built at distances sufficient to deny close neighbours, although there was still the feeling of belonging to a community, and only one of them was exempt from Signora Vincente's fund of gossipy stories about the little community.

The exception was the largest of all the villas, the one she was approaching at the moment, and even the Signora had not yet penetrated its suggestion of cloistered grandeur, nor any of her friends apparently. It was perhaps its air of secret seclusion that always fascinated Rosalind, for she had never seen anyone either enter or leave it while she was passing and the guard of dark cypress that surrounded it discouraged idle curiosity.

The Villa Mimosa stood on the steep terraced cliffs like a palace among its more humble neighbours, big and creamy-white and somehow arrogant amid its beautiful gardens, different from the rest of the villas and intriguing because of its suggestion of isolation.

Rosalind had once or twice thought of standing at the end of that curved, tree-lined avenue and really taking a good look at the house, but so far her natural reserve had deterred her. Obviously it was owned by someone with wealth enough to maintain it, for it showed no sign of neglect, as one or two of the others did.

It was not simply the size of the villa that attracted her, but the sense of grandeur it possessed. It belonged to the Mendori family, that much Signora Vincente knew, but she had been so vague when Rosalind had ventured to mention it that it was plain she knew little or nothing about it or its occupants.

Still intent on enjoying her view of the bay and the lush terraces below her, she was oblivious of everything else, even the sound of an approaching car coming from the motorway at a speed that was reckless and dangerous on such a narrow road.

The first she realised of its proximity was when a

9

blast from a strident horn and a screeching of tyres on the road sent her leaping for the safety of a stone wall bordering the narrow pathway. Breathing rapidly, she gazed at the offender with wide startled eyes.

The car was a big, shiny dark Mercedes and it came to a halt only a few feet from where she stood, sending up a fine cloud of dust as it braked. The driver got out, not bothering that his vehicle completely blocked the road to other traffic, and came hurrying back towards her, his hands already making gestures of apology, while Rosalind watched him dazedly.

She had seen many good-looking men since coming to Italy, but the driver of the Mercedes was exceptionally handsome and she found it impossible to be as angry as her instinct told her she should be. He was a little more than medium height and slim, with the sleek healthy look of one who lives well, and his dark eyes expressed more than anxiety as he came towards her. They glowed with a frank appreciation that she had become used to in the eyes of the village men, only somehow the expression was much more disturbing when combined with such staggering good looks.

He spread his eloquent hands, and his broad shoulders, in a grey shantung jacket, lifted expressively in regret. '*Sono molto dispiacente, signorina!*' he said. His voice was deep and had a reasonant quality that Rosalind found very pleasant and he was studying her again with his dark eyes narrowed briefly and curiously. From the top of her pale gold head to her small sandalled feet she was subjected to an intense and obviously expert scrutiny, then he bobbed his head in a slight bow. 'The *signorina* is English?' he asked, and Rosalind, still in something of a daze, nodded.

'Yes, I'm English,' she agreed.

She was unsure just what to make of him, but it was easy to see he was impressed by what he saw, though having him standing there on the public road making his approval so obvious was rather disconcerting. He was smiling, as if he was well pleased with his own deduction, and Rosalind could not help smiling in return.

He was what she had always thought of as typically Italian, with a smooth olive-brown complexion and thick black hair and, of course, those expressive dark eyes that were still regarding her with bold appreciation. He seemed to have charm and self-confidence in plenty, even a certain arrogance, but the charm was uppermost and it would be difficult to snub such a man, no matter what he did.

'Ah, *signorina*,' he said, gazing at her with a look that defied anyone to blame him. 'How can I apologise for almost running you down? It was *criminale*, forgive me, *per piacere*!'

Rosalind shook her head. It was impossible to put all the blame on to him, although her first instinct had been to do so. He had been driving much too fast for the state of the road, but she had been wandering rather, her mind on the scenery instead of on the approach of traffic.

'Please,' she said, sounding a little breathless, 'I was to blame too. I wasn't keeping my mind on the road, or the possibility of something coming.' She felt a disturbing sense of excitement when she met the boldness of his eyes again, and hastily looked away.

'You are kind as well as beautiful, *signorina*,' he said in that fascinating voice. '*Grazie!*'

Whoever he was, he seemed much more intent on furthering their acquaintance than in going on his way, and Rosalind could not find it in her heart to simply walk off and leave him. 'I'm afraid I was admiring the view instead of looking where I was going,' she told him, and he turned and looked down at the scene below. The tiny bay, shimmering in the sun and the narrow, sunny quay where the fishing boats waited for the evening tide.

'You like Crisdorfi, *signorina*?' he asked, turning back to her, and she nodded. There was a frankly speculative look in the dark eyes that gave Rosalind a small, pleasurable thrill as she hastily avoided looking directly at him. 'You are staying here?' he asked, without giving her time to answer his first question. 'On *vacanza*, perhaps?'

Rosalind nodded. 'I'm here for two weeks,' she told him, and took a moment to wonder at her own reactions. Her usually well controlled emotions were stirring uneasily, and she could only blame it on the Italian sun and on the dark eyes of the man before her. 'It isn't very long,' she added, 'and I only wish I had more time here—it's beautiful.'

Her companion inclined his head briefly. '*Molto*

bella!' he murmured, and it was evident from the look in his eyes that he assigned the compliment to herself rather than to the view. Rosalind's heart was doing strange and inexplicable things suddenly, and she almost laughed aloud to think of herself being so blatantly and easily disarmed by this young Italian with his seductive voice. A quick glance at her hands confirmed the absence of a ring on her left hand, and a dark brow arched enquiringly. 'The *signorina* is alone?' he asked, and Rosalind debated whether it was wise to admit it, but some unfamiliar devil at her elbow decided the matter for her, and she nodded almost without realising it.

'I'm staying with Signora Vincente,' she told him, 'at the Villa Gardina, just below here.'

'Ah!' A beam of pleasure glowed in the dark eyes. 'Then perhaps, *signorina,* you will allow me to show you more of our beautiful coast while you are here?' he suggested blandly.

'That's very kind of you, *signore.*' She was unsure just what she was letting herself in for, but there was always the homely figure of Signora Vincente somewhere comfortingly close if she got out of her depth, and she found it hard to resist this man.

'You are staying very close to my own home, *signorina,*' he told her, waving a vague hand in the direction of the road behind him. 'Allow me to introduce myself—I am Luigi Mendori of the Villa Mimosa, which is a little way from where we stand now!'

The Villa Mimosa! Rosalind could not help being impressed, although she tried not to show it. There were indications, of course, that this charming stranger was no plain man in the street. That big, shiny car he drove and the impeccably tailored suit, even his air of self-confidence, spoke of a position in society that was among the privileged and the wealthy. It made her nervous for a second to realise that probably a wealthy young man would be more inclined to indulge in casual affairs because he could afford to take his choice but, despite his bold, confident manner, there was something about this man that appealed to her, and she extended a slim hand and smiled.

'I'm Rosalind Matthews,' she said.

'Rosalinda?' Once more she coped with pulses that were suddenly and inexplicably much too fast, while he held her hand for much longer than was strictly necessary. He gave her name an Italian accent too which made it sound quite lyrically beautiful, and she was almost ashamed of the flutter of excitement he caused when he raised her hand and pressed his lips to her fingers before releasing it. 'It also is beautiful, *signorina*!'

'It's very old-fashioned,' Rosalind said, and laughed a little light-headedly. 'My mother chose it from one of Shakespeare's plays.'

'Signor Shakespeare would have been honoured, Signorina Rosalinda!'

The dark eyes gave promise of all kinds of impossible things and Rosalind pulled herself up sharply as she met their expressive gaze head on.

14

She told herself she was being silly to allow his outrageous flattery to go to her head, but it was difficult to simply accept it without being affected. The trouble was that Luigi Mendori was quite unlike any other man she had met, and she frankly enjoyed the sensation he created, no matter how foolish she might prove to be.

It was in an attempt to be more level-headed that she glanced at her wristwatch. Not only was the time getting on, but Luigi Mendori's big car was still blocking the narrow road and she was unwilling to be caught up in one of the emotional and garrulous scenes that such an incident could cause between Italian drivers. Reluctantly she decided to bring the encounter to an end and she smiled up at him apologetically.

'I really should go, Signor Mendori,' she said. 'Signora Vincente is expecting me back for lunch, and——'

'You must go so soon?' Expressive Latin shoulders made a tragedy of their parting, and he looked at her with all the sadness in the world in his dark eyes. 'But it is such a pity, *signorina*, when we have only now met!'

'I'm sorry,' Rosalind said, and once more that unfamiliar devil at her elbow prompted her so that she looked up at him through her thick lashes. 'I've enjoyed meeting you, *signore*.'

Luigi Mendori seized her hand, holding it lightly in his while his fingers squeezed hers gently. 'I shall make it my affair to see that we meet again, you may be sure of it, *signorina*,' he told her earnestly, and his warm brown eyes glowed in a way that sent a small shiver along Rosalind's spine as he bowed over her hand once more. 'But—since you must go, *addio*, Signorina Rosalinda!' Once more his lips brushed warmly against her fingers and her heart fluttered warningly.

'Goodbye, Signor Mendori,' she said, and wondered if it was goodbye or if she would ever see him again.

Having raised the subject of Luigi Mendori with her hostess, Rosalind discovered that Signora Vincente knew a little about him, although nothing about the rest of the Mendori family, and her knowledge of Luigi amounted to no more than Rosalind could have guessed from her own meeting with him.

He was a young man with more than his share of good looks and wealthy enough to indulge his taste for expensive cars and beautiful women. Signora Vincente, Rosalind suspected, read more into her accidental meeting with her new acquaintance than she let on, and when she brought the news the following morning that Signor Mendori was asking for her on the telephone, she was smiling broadly and using her eyes to great effect.

Rosalind took the call with a nervous flutter in her stomach, and she gave her name hesitantly. Luigi Mendori's attractive voice was unmistakable and, as at their first meeting, she found herself responding to it with a sudden sense of excitement. 'Ah, Signorina Matthews!' He sounded rather as if

16

he was trying to talk without being overheard, and Rosalind wondered why. 'Luigi Mendori, *signorina*, you remember me?' he asked, and Rosalind smiled faintly to herself. It was unlikely that any woman would forget meeting Luigi Mendori and he would be fully aware of the fact.

'Yes, of course I remember you, Signor Mendori,' she said, and heard his murmur of satisfaction. 'Good morning.'

'*Buon giorno, signorina!*' He hesitated, and again Rosalind had the feeling that he was making sure he was not overheard. '*Signorina*,' he said after a moment, 'you are here, in Crisdorfi on a *vacanza*, no? A *vacanza* from your employment?'

'Yes, that's right,' she agreed, and frowned. Something in his voice, in his manner, puzzled her and she could not imagine why it did, or why he was asking such questions of her. 'Signor Mendori,' she said, 'I don't know——'

'Ah, you are—puzzled, *sì*?' he asked, and laughed softly. Rosalind could imagine those well tailored shoulders shrugging in a gesture of regret for having confused her. 'But of course, *signorina*, I am sorry!'

'Oh, it's all right,' Rosalind assured him, 'but I am a bit puzzled, as you say.' She was undecided whether to be more wary or curious about his questioning her. 'I don't quite see why you're interested, that's all,' she explained, and laughed a little uneasily. 'It's nothing secret that I'm here on holiday, of course, but——'

'But you cannot understand why I, a stranger,

should concern myself with your reasons for being here, hmm?' He gave her no time to reply, but went on. 'It is because I have an idea that concerns you,' he said. '*Capisce, signorina?*'

'An idea? I don't think I understand, *signore*.' She was aware that Signora Vincente was taking more than a casual interest, even though she was ostensibly clearing away their breakfast things, and she wondered if the smile she wore was because she knew the identity of the caller and thought she knew why he was calling. Signora Vincente, she recalled, had been impressed by her meeting with Luigi Mendori.

'You have told me that you like it here in Crisdorfi,' he went on. 'That you would like to stay longer, *si?*' Once more he gave her no time to answer, but laughed as if he could well imagine her confusion. 'Forgive me, *signorina*,' he begged, 'but I am trying to—how is it you say?—fix things up for you!'

'Fix things up?'

He dismissed her obvious confusion with a laugh, and it was obvious when he spoke again that he had made up his mind at last. 'If you wish to stay in Crisdorfi,' he said, 'I have the means to achieve this, *signorina*. If you will call here at the Villa Mimosa it is possible that you may stay.'

'I could——' Rosalind's voice failed her.

Her brain was spinning with the very idea of being able to stay in a place as idyllic as Crisdorfi, but heaven knew what Luigi Mendori had in mind when he suggested it. 'You would like to work here?' his voice broke into her stunned silence, and it was obvious that he already knew the answer.

'Oh, yes, of course, I'd love to stay, but——'

Once more she stopped in mid-sentence, unable to find the right words. She would love to stay on, of course, but there were considerations, things she would need to know before she took such an irrevocable step, and it was all happening rather too quickly for her to think clearly.

She could hardly be employed in her usual capacity without some knowledge of Italian, and that left only domestic work as far as she could see, something she was in two minds about. Also there was the question of what else would be involved if she worked for a man like Luigi Mendori. He was charming and flattering, but to be employed by him would create a whole new situation.

She was a good secretary, four years at secretarial college had made sure of that, but domestic work was a little out of her line. She was a capable enough cook when she needed to be, and ordinary housework was not beyond her, but she had never considered making it a career. All that and much more was going through her mind while Luigi Mendori waited at the other end of the line.

'*Signorina?*' His voice brought her swiftly back from speculation and the need to find an answer. 'You will come?' he asked, and Rosalind hesitated only a moment longer.

'Very well, Signor Mendori,' she said impulsively. 'I'll come and see you!' She was probably being very rash, perhaps even foolhardy, but she was following her heart instead of her head, and the satisfaction it gave her was surprising.

'*Buono!*' She could imagine his smile and the gleam of satisfaction in those dark eyes. 'If you will arrive here in about one hour, *signorina*,' he told her, 'I will do my best to see that you have your wish to stay come true.'

Rosalind was already feeling faintly alarmed at her own impulsiveness. She had a perfectly good job back in England, a job she quite enjoyed, despite occàsional bouts of boredom, but the temptation of being able to stay in Crisdorfi had simply been too much to resist. Pehaps it was not too late, perhaps if she spoke up now, changed her mind.

'Signor Mendori!' She spoke hastily, for he was already about to hang up. 'Perhaps I've been a bit—hasty.'

'Ah, *signorina!*' His attractive voice throbbed with disappointment and she had to believe he felt the way he sounded. 'You will come, *per piacere!* You will not have other thoughts, I will be desolate!'

Signora Vincente passed her in the hall and she glanced at her, almost apologetically as she struggled with her decision. 'Very well, *signore*,' she said, a little breathlessly. 'I'll be there in about an hour.'

'Ah, *buono!*' His sigh was deep and the laughter that followed soft and well satisfied. '*A più tarde, signorina. Addio!*'

It had occurred to Rosalind, as she got herself

ready, to ask if Signora Vincente would go with her to the Villa Mimosa, but then she decided that she was perfectly capable of handling the interview alone. She still had some doubts, but she dismissed them impatiently and instead thought of the pleasure of living and working in Crisdorfi.

She did not know, she realised as she looked at her reflection and frowned, whether or not there was a Signora Mendori. Luigi Mendori had not mentioned a wife or a mother, but there had scarcely been time during their very brief acquaintance to learn anything about each other. In fact the more she looked at the situation in the cold light of reason, the more incredible her own actions seemed.

She shrugged uneasily as she gave her hair a last vigorous brush and looked again at her reflection with critical eyes. A plain turquoise blue dress in soft terylene suited her colouring perfectly and was not too frivolous for an interview. The fitted bodice outlined her excellent figure, it was true, but the neckline was decorously high and it had short sleeves.

Picking up her handbag, she took a last look in the mirror, then turned to go. Her heart was rapping hard at her ribs, for heaven knew what she was letting herself in for, but it was too late to have second thoughts now, and to be quite honest she quite enjoyed the excitement of the unknown.

The Villa Mimosa was approached via a long tree-lined drive and Rosalind walked between the dark plumes of cypress feeling rather more nervous than when she set out. Her cheeks were flushed, partly because she had hurried, mistakenly thinking she was late, when in fact she was about a quarter of an hour earlier than she need have been, and there was a dark look in her eyes that made them appear more violet than blue.

The villa itself was even more attractive close to, and she took the opportunity to admire it as she walked towards a wide porch sheltering the wide open doors. Built of the same yellow-white stone as most of the other villas, the Villa Mimosa had a mellowness that suggested age and was beautiful and quite distinctive, its outline softened by the riot of flowers, shrubs and trees that grew all round it.

Beyond the avenue of cypress there were orange and lemon trees and the same sweet familiar scent that permeated the lower cliffs where the Villa Gardina was. Roses and the ubiquitous bougainvillaea trailed over the creamy walls, and big stone jars held musky-scented geraniums of scarlet, pink and white.

The fluffy yellow mimosa that gave it its name flourished in huge showers of bloom beside the open doors and filled the air around it with its sweet, peppery scent. There was the same dreamlike, slightly unreal quality about it that there was about Crisdorfi as a whole and Rosalind thought it was beautiful. How could anyone refuse the opportunity to live and work there?

The air was warm and perfumed like incense as she stepped on to the porch and the thought of working in such a place was irresistible. For all her delight in her surroundings her heart was thudding heavily in her breast at the sound of her own footsteps on the tiled mosaic and her head spun with anticipation of the unknown.

She looked for a bell pull and found an ornately carved bronze satyr leering from a stone niche beside the door. Its appearance deterred her for a moment from using it, and before she could reach out, the appearance of a manservant made her action unnecessary. He was short and stockily built and dressed in a suit of royal blue with silver buttons, and the sight of the livery caused Rosalind another moment's misgiving, for it suggested living on a much grander scale than anything she was used to.

The man looked at her for a moment with hooded dark eyes that had the same glow of appreciation she had seen so often in the eyes of the young men on the quay. Then he inclined his head enquiringly and raised his brows.

'*Signorina?*' he enquired, making it fairly obvious that he was not expecting her, and Rosalind felt a curl of embarrassment for a moment.

'My name is Matthews,' she ventured after a moment of indecision, and hoping he spoke at least some English. 'Rosalind Matthews—I believe Mr. Mendori is expecting me. Signor Mendori,' she added explicitly, to be sure she had been understood.

The man looked at her curiously for a moment, then inclined his head and stepped back to allow her to enter. '*Signorina!*'

Indicating that she should follow him, he made his way across a huge hall, nodding his head briefly as if he realised how nervous she felt suddenly and wondered why she was there. The hall, as much as Rosalind had time to see of it as they made their leisurely progress, was a revelation to her. Accustomed as she was to Signora Vincente's more humble villa, it was palatial and there seemed to be a strangely exciting, almost sensual air about it that was both pleasing and a little disquieting.

In her present, uncharacteristic mood she was startled to find her reactions much different from her more normal cool control. Italy and its people were having the most curious effect on her and sometimes she surprised herself. At other times she would probably have dismissed such a place as being ostentatious, now she accepted it as different from anything she had ever known before, but beautiful for all that.

A frieze of gilded alabaster figures decorated the high ceiling where it joined with white walls, figures of men and women, lightly clad and obviously indulging in the most worldly of pleasures. The artistry was exquisite and the whole work beautiful, but Rosalind, even in her present mood, also found it oddly disturbing and she kept her eyes lowered as she followed the manservant to a door at the other end of the hall.

She had time to register, too, a long grey marble staircase to one side of the hall and a sweeping curved gallery glimpsed at through a high arch at the top of the stairs. Her guide opened the door and ushered her into what seemed to be a *salon*, and just as rich-looking as the hall she had just come through. Everything, it seemed, was on a grand scale in the Villa Mimosa.

The room was long and wide and carpeted in a deep moss green, and its ceiling too was decorated in a similar fashion to the one in the hall, except that here the gilded figures were engaged in hunting deer and wild boar. Gilt-framed paintings in rich oils hung at intervals around the white walls, portraying handsome, black-eyed men and equally handsome women. All of them had that same look of autocracy that she had noted in Luigi Mendori, and she had no hesitation in recognising them as past generations of Mendoris.

A huge Venetian mirror hung above the marble fireplace and reflected the whole room in reverse, including her own diminutive figure standing in the centre of the green carpet and looking completely out of place and rather vulnerable.

'Be seated, *signorina*, *per piacere*,' the man-servant told her, and indicated one of the heavy gilded chairs that furnished the room. 'I will inform Signor Mendori of your presence.' He inclined his head briefly in a bow and once more the dark, explicit eyes expressed appreciation of her fairness. '*Mi scusi, signorina.*'

CHAPTER TWO

ROSALIND had been alone for only a few moments when she heard the sound of voices outside in the hall. She was almost sure she recognised one of them as Luigi Mendori's, but identification was made difficult because both voices had the same depth and resonance. The difference was that one of them seemed to suggest that the owner was angry and impatient, and that, Rosalind thought, did not fit in with the character of Luigi Mendori as she saw him. He had seemed much too light-hearted to give way to temper as this man was.

Whoever the two men were, they seemed to be arguing about something, although the exchange was short and in Italian so that she could gather nothing from what she heard. The discourse continued for only a few seconds and then footsteps could be heard coming briskly in the direction of the room where she sat, a little apprehensive, on the very edge of her chair.

The door opened so abruptly that she got to her feet almost involuntarily and stared at the man who came in. He was not Luigi Mendori, she was certain of that, although there was a basic resemblance to the man she had met yesterday. There seemed little doubt that he was the other man involved in the argument, for he still had a brittle air of anger about him, but more than that, his personality was such that she stared, feeling herself trembling even before he spoke.

He was slightly taller than Luigi Mendori and probably several years older too, but he was much less conventionally handsome. There was a strong, almost barbaric magnetism about him that stunned her senses so that she felt at a complete loss as she stared at him, her usual self-control completely deserting her.

He had the same black hair and smooth golden-brown skin as Luigi Mendori, but his eyes were black rather than merely dark and his chiselled features reminded her suddenly and uneasily of the disturbing bronze satyr in the stone niche outside. A face that was hard to forget and stunningly exciting to be faced with unexpectedly.

His mouth, wide and slightly crooked, had a tight stern look, and there was a deep cleft in the square chin below a strong Roman nose, all of which added up to an overall impression of vigorous, ruthless masculinity. Rosalind had thought Luigi Mendori's manner suggested inborn pride, but this man left her in no doubt; he had an arrogance that delegated all other men to a lower plane, and yet for all that he was devastatingly attractive.

He wore white from head to toe, including a kind of tunic that buttoned high at the neck and gave him a military look, and it took Rosalind a moment or two to recognise the semi-uniform usually worn for fencing. Pausing briefly in the doorway he subjected her to a long, explicit scrutiny that set the blood racing wildly through her veins and brought a swift flush of colour to her cheeks, then he strode towards her in long, silent strides, watching her as he came.

'You are Miss Matthews?' he asked, and Rosalind frowned at the way he asked the question, even though she nodded agreement. His tone seemed to suggest that she was not only an intruder but an unwelcome one.

'I'm Rosalind Matthews,' she agreed, her heart fluttering anxiously as she sought to identify him. Judging by his manner he was of some importance in the household. 'I came to see Signor Mendori,' she told him, 'at his request.'

Rosalind curled her fingers tightly into her palms in an instinctive gesture of defence when he came and stood directly in front of her. He was an overpowering man in every sense of the word and she found him incredibly disturbing—a sensation she disliked.

'I am Mendori,' he told her. 'Lucifer Mendori—my manservant told me that you wished to see me, but I believe now that there has been some misunderstanding. It was my brother you expected to see, *signorina*, was it not?'

His English was perfect, though rather pedantic, and much less frequently sprinkled with Italian than his brother's had been, and Rosalind looked at him in some confusion. 'I didn't realise,' she said. 'I mean it was Signor Luigi Mendori that I wanted to see. I didn't realise he had a brother.'

'I am the elder brother,' Lucifer Mendori informed her. 'You should have been more fully informed, *signorina*.' The black eyes swept over her in a brief but frank appraisal and once more Rosalind felt a prickle of resentment at his manner towards her. 'When you enquired for Signor Mendori naturally Adolfo assumed that you wished to see me—my brother is referred to as Signor Luigi.'

'Oh, I see; I'm sorry.' It was easy to see how the mistake had occurred, but what still puzzled her was why, when she had heard Luigi Mendori out there in the hall, he had not come in himself to see her instead of leaving her to face this discomfiting brother of his. She glanced at the door behind him. 'Didn't I hear him—Signor Luigi, just now?' she asked. 'If you——'

'At the moment you are in my hands, *signorina*,' he interrupted coolly but firmly, and Rosalind drew an involuntary breath. 'I have been given some indication of why you are here.'

It would be difficult to simply walk out now, Rosalind thought, and tell him that she had made a mistake in coming to the Villa Mimosa in the first place, but she was tempted to do just that. There was something about Lucifer Mendori that she found oddly disquieting, but at the same time he fascinated her as no man ever had before on such short acquaintance—even his good-looking brother. The resultant emotional chaos was something quite new to her, and her present instinct was to escape from something she felt she might live to regret before long.

'Perhaps if Signor Luigi is busy,' she said, sounding much more nervous than she had hoped, 'I should come back some other time.'

The way to the door was blocked by his tall, stern figure directly in front of her and she could not quite bring herself to just brush past him and make a purposeful exit. Instead she stood there, still curious and not a little intrigued as to why he had decided to see her himself rather than simply have the servant inform her that Luigi was busy. There was something infinitely suggestive about the way he was looking at her, and yet Rosalind could not yet determine why it was.

'You have only recently met my brother, *signorina*,' he said, and did not even bother to phrase it as a question.

'That's right,' Rosalind agreed. She was appalled, when it came to putting it into words, just how flimsy her reasons sounded for coming to the house of a complete stranger, alone. 'I met Signor Luigi yesterday,' she said, and would have gone on to explain the circumstances, but he gave her no chance.

'Only yesterday?' An arched brow suggested that his worst fears had been confirmed, and Rosalind flushed.

'Perhaps it was a little rash of me to come here like this,' she admitted defensively, 'but Signor Luigi said that there might be a job for me here.'

'You are looking for employment?'

He sounded as if he doubted her, and Rosalind fought hard to remain cool and calm, but it was incredibly difficult when she was faced with a man like Lucifer Mendori. She was not, strictly speaking, looking for employment in the way he probably meant it, but to admit that she already had a job to go back to would inevitably give him the wrong idea of her reasons for being there.

'At the moment I'm actually on holiday, Signor Mendori,' she explained as coolly as possible in the circumstances. 'I have a job in England, but I happened to mention to Signor Luigi that I'd love to stay on here if I could, and he must have remembered what I said, although it wasn't really a serious statement at the time. Then, when your brother rang me and said there *might* be work for me here—well, I was intrigued enough to come and see what it was at least.'

'And also, of course, to see my brother again,' Lucifer Mendori suggested quietly.

'No—not necessarily!'

Rosalind denied it vehemently, but she knew it was more than half true—she had been hoping to see Luigi Mendori again. Her self-control, she realised with dismay, was fast disappearing in the face of this man's disturbing personality, and she had no doubt that he saw her simply as an English visitor looking for a little Latin romance while she was on holiday.

'Forgive me if I have doubts, *signorina*,' he said, 'but are you trying to tell me that you would willingly have gone alone to any house in Crisdorfi simply because some strange man asked you to?' The voice was quiet, but it suggested not only disbelief but a certain contempt, and the black eyes glittered a challenge which she met uneasily.

'You may check with your brother, *signore*,' she told him, shaky-voiced. 'He will confirm that I agreed to come here only after some persuasion and the assurance that there was the chance of a job.'

A black brow arched in comment on the necessity of persuasion where his brother was concerned. 'Luigi is handsome, so I have always believed,' he said, 'and wealthy too. Is that not persuasion enough, *signorina*?'

Rosalind thrust out her chin, her eyes darkly angry. 'You seem to be labouring under a delusion concerning me,' she said. 'You seem to think I'm some kind of——' She waved her hands helplessly, failing to find the words she wanted. 'Well, you're quite wrong, *signore*! Signor Luigi Mendori almost ran me down in his car yesterday and he stopped to apologise; after that we talked for a few moments, that's all!'

Once more that appraising glance swept over her, and a hint of movement tipped one corner of his mouth briefly. 'But Luigi of course was not prepared to let matters end with an apology,' he guessed. 'You are very beautiful, and he can never resist beautiful women!'

It was less a compliment than a statement, made in that cool, detached voice, Rosalind recognised, and again she felt her anger rising, resenting his cool confidence in summarising the situation as he saw it. It would be so much better all round if she could escape from what had become an embarrassing situation, as soon as possible, and from this disturbing man in particular.

It was with the idea of escape in mind that she gripped her handbag more firmly and prepared to depart with as much of her self-possession intact as possible. 'I can see that coming here was an embarrassing mistake, Signor Mendori,' she said, 'I apologise for troubling you, but my mistake was genuine; no matter what you think, I had no ulterior motive! I won't bother you any further—good morning!'

She gave him as wide a berth as possible when she walked past him, but even so that powerful, aggressive personality seemed to reach out and envelop her, so that she came abruptly to a halt when he spoke. '*Signorina!*' Rosalind turned, her eyes shining resentfully, and he met her gaze as if he knew exactly how she was feeling. 'My brother took more upon himself than he was entitled to do,' he said in his pure, pedantic English. 'I can understand your feelings, *signorina.*'

'Can you?' It was difficult not to be outright rude to him, but she was still influenced by that irresistible personality.

'Luigi should not have persuaded you to come when he had no authority to do so,' he told her.

So that was it, Rosalind thought dizzily. He considered himself undisputed head of his household and he disliked his younger brother taking things upon himself. Luigi had probably met him in the hall and given him some idea of what he had in mind. Seeing her as an opportunist, Lucifer Mendori had taken it upon himself to put her firmly in her place, and had autocratically dismissed his brother.

What startled Rosalind was the fact that she

33

could see how it might look to him and, in the circumstances, she could not entirely blame him if he objected to his brother trying to staff the villa with his casual paramours. 'Please, Signor Mendori,' she said, 'don't say any more about it. It was a mistake to come here, I can see that, and I'm sorry you've been inconvenienced.'

There was a strange sense of dissatisfaction about walking away from the situation, and yet there was little else she could do now, but as she turned to leave Lucifer Mendori spoke again. 'May I ask what qualifications you have, *signorina*?' he asked, and Rosalind stared at him, her heart pounding uneasily in her breast as she shook her head.

'It doesn't matter, Signor Mendori,' she said, 'if you don't——'

Lucifer Mendori cut her short, one large hand waving her impatiently to silence. 'You spoke of seeking employment here, *signorina*,' he reminded her, and Rosalind nodded absently.

'I did,' she agreed, 'but you said——'

'I said nothing on the matter of employing you,' he told her coolly. 'I merely informed you that my brother was not authorised to promise you work here. It is my decision whether or not you are suitable and I shall not take you into my household simply because you have a beautiful face, *signorina*. I leave such foolishness to Luigi!'

Rosalind stared at him, her heart beating with such breathless urgency that it was making her head spin. She still resented his manner, but it was not simply resentment that stirred in her as she

34

looked at that arrogant, bronze satyr's face, it was a curious sense of excitement at the thought of working for him. It would not be easy, but it could be rewarding, and she found herself wanting to convince him of her suitability more than anything at the moment.

'You—you mean there really *is* a job?' she asked, and Lucifer Mendori regarded her steadily for a moment.

'That depends upon your answer regarding what qualifications you have, *signorina*,' he said.

Rosalind gathered her wits together hastily. 'I'm a secretary,' she told him breathlessly. 'I trained at a London secretarial college and stayed for a while on the staff there. I've been with my present firm for about a year now.'

Thick black lashes half concealed his eyes as he looked down at her in silence. For some strange reason he seemed to find her answer suspect, although she could not imagine why. 'Did my brother indicate what kind of employment was available, Miss Matthews?' he asked quietly, and Rosalind shook her head.

'No, Signor Mendori.'

'Then what made you think you might find work as a secretary in this house, *signorina*?'

It was plain, of course, he was still not entirely convinced about her, and she sighed inwardly. 'I didn't know,' she told him. 'I didn't know what Signor Luigi had in mind, but it didn't really matter. I wasn't averse to changing my job if it gave me the opportunity to stay on in Crisdorfi for a while.' Immediately she saw that her answer left her wide open to suspicion that Luigi was her reason for wanting to stay on, and she shook her head hastily. 'It's just that I've never worked abroad before,' she explained, 'and I don't mind making a temporary change if it gives me a chance to work in Italy.'

He studied her closely for a second, then indicated with one hand that she should sit down again, although he remained standing himself, his hands behind him, clasped together and drawing back his shoulders until the white tunic was pulled taut across his broad chest. There was a small frown pulling his black brows together, as if he was giving serious consideration to the matter in hand, and Rosalind perched once more on the edge of one of the big gilded chairs.

She sat rather primly, with her hands in her lap and her eyes downcast, while her heart tapped away anxiously at her ribs, and from the shadow of her lashes she watched him. Something had made him change his mind about her. Had made him decide that she was not just seeking a brief holiday affair with his good-looking brother, and she wondered what it was.

He took a box of long, slim cheroots from a pocket and lit one, the flame of the lighter casting shadows on his cheekbones and that proud Roman nose, and giving an almost unholy glow to his black eyes, so that Rosalind was again reminded of the bronze satyr outside by the door. The comparison disturbed her, and yet it was not altogether an unpleasant sensation when a shiver slid along her spine as she watched him.

'You do not speak or write in Italian?' he asked, so suddenly that Rosalind was obliged to snatch herself hastily back from the uneasy fantasy, and she stared at him for a second before she answered.

'No,' she said. 'No, I'm afraid I don't, Signor Mendori.'

She expected him to dismiss her out of hand after she made the admission, but instead he merely pursed his lips. 'It is no matter for the time being,' he said, and shrugged his broad shoulders. Drawing deeply on the cheroot, he exhaled a stream of blue smoke that partially hid his features from her as he spoke. 'I am prepared to offer you a position here, Miss Matthews,' he said. 'That is if you are serious about your desire to work in Italy.'

'Oh, but of course I am!' Rosalind assured him hastily. 'As long as it's something I can do, of course,' she added with a cautious smile. 'I'm not too helpless about most things.'

'I understood you to say that you were a fully trained secretary!' His voice was sharp and Rosalind looked at him for a moment, hoping she was not misunderstanding him.

'You—you mean it's a secretarial job?' she asked. 'Oh, but that's wonderful!'

Lucifer Mendori regarded her for a moment through a haze of blue smoke, and that arrogant aggressiveness reached out to envelop her again, so that her heart fluttered uneasily. 'You would have taken domestic work?' he asked, and Rosalind shrugged, unsure just what she would have done when it came to the point.

'It would have depended on what it was,' she admitted. 'I'm not trained for domestic work, but I might have managed some jobs, I imagine.'

Briefly the wide mouth crooked into a ghost of a smile and he shook his head slowly as he looked down at her. 'I cannot see you in the part of domestic servant,' he said quietly, and Rosalind felt herself blushing. 'You are not easily—subservient, *signorina*, am I right?'

'Am I expected to be?' she asked impulsively, and he did not immediately answer, but regarded her steadily, as if speculating on just how willing a servant she would make.

'Your question serves to prove my point,' he told her. 'You do not take easily to being given instructions, and that *will* be required of you, *signorina*. It remains to be seen whether or not you are willing to submit to the routine required of my household.'

Rosalind looked up at him, her heart thudding at her ribs with head-spinning urgency. She was increasingly aware every minute of the strength of his personality and the sheer physical presence of the man. Everything about him suggested a hard ruthless character, and yet something, somewhere, gave a hint of something more human and exciting.

His body had a lean, hard look and his hands, large and strong, suggested at once both gentleness and violence—a disturbing observation that she quelled hastily, because there was enough about

Lucifer Mendori that was disturbing, without discovering more. As a man he was devastatingly attractive, but as a character he was so far an unknown quantity, and she found the challenge of getting to know him irresistible.

His voice brought her swiftly out of her uneasy speculation, and she tried to concentrate on what he was saying. 'I have in mind the post of secretary-companion,' he told her. 'Would you be capable of performing both those duties, Miss Matthews?'

'Secretary-companion?' Rosalind stared at him for a second or two, startled by the information, for she could not easily imagine what the second part of the title implied as far as Lucifer Mendori was concerned.

'Are you capable of performing the duties required for such a position?' he insisted, and there was a suggestion of impatience in his voice so that Rosalind nodded hastily.

'Oh, yes, I think so,' she said, unwilling to admit that she had doubts. 'I don't know exactly what's expected of me as a companion—I mean, I've always thought of companions as for——'

'My grandmother, the Contessa Mendori, is the one who requires your services,' he told her, and Rosalind would have sworn that she caught a glimpse of amusement in his eyes as she blinked in surprise. 'Do you imagine that I have need of a paid companion, *signorina*?' he enquired, and she felt the warmth of colour in her cheeks again.

'Oh, no, of course not!' she denied.

'My grandmother has a number of friends

abroad with whom she communicates in both English and French,' Lucifer Mendori told her. 'An increasing infirmity makes handwriting difficult for her, therefore there is a need for someone to do the correspondence for her. Do you perhaps speak some French, Miss Matthews?'

'Some,' Rosalind admitted, a little dazedly. 'I write it quite well, and I'm sure I could cope.'

The black eyes regarded her steadily for a moment, narrowed slightly and shadowed by long, thick black lashes. 'Can you also—cope with my brother's constant presence, *signorina?*' he asked, and Rosalind nodded, though a little less certainly.

It would be difficult with Luigi Mendori in the house, to give her whole attention to the correspondence of an old lady, and perhaps even more difficult to cope with his elder brother's virile and disturbing presence, but she was prepared to try. 'I can cope,' she said, and after a few seconds Lucifer Mendori nodded.

'Then you have the position, Miss Matthews,' he said. 'Subject, of course, to the Contessa's approval.'

'Of course.' Rosalind curled her hands tightly over her handbag and looked up at him. 'Thank you, Signor Mendori.'

It was hard not to dismiss the whole thing as a dream inspired by the heady scent of the lemon trees, and from which she would presently wake, Rosalind thought, but Lucifer Mendori was no figment of her imagination. He was undeniably a creature of flesh and blood, a man of such sensuous arrogance that she found it hard to remain cool and controlled in his presence. Such a man would make working for him a constant battle of emotions, even if she was more closely concerned with his grandmother, but she was surprisingly ready to take on whatever crises occurred.

'You are prepared to commence your duties at once?' he said, but once more she realised that the question was merely a formality—he did not seriously expect her to refuse.

Nevertheless, she hesitated, for she ought really to give her present employer more notice than a letter in the post telling him that she had found herself another job in Italy, but she could not bear to think of this opportunity slipping through her fingers. 'I—yes, I could,' she said a little dazedly, and Lucifer Mendori frowned. 'I'm still officially on holiday from my present firm,' she explained, 'but——'

'My requirement is immediate, *signorina*!' The deep, firm voice cut short her explanation, and he expelled a long plume of blue smoke from his lips, looking at her through its haze. 'If you are having reservations about working for me——'

'Oh, no, I haven't!' Rosalind assured him hastily. 'I can start whenever you like!'

'*Benissimo!*' He nodded his head as if he considered the whole matter concluded to his satisfaction. Bending to put out the cheroot, he came within touching distance and Rosalind almost jumped back instinctively, for there was a warm, voluptuous aura about him that shivered through her when the heat of his body enveloped her. 'You

41

will be here by ten o'clock tomorrow morning, *signorina*,' he said as he straightened up, and Rosalind stared at him.

'Tomorrow morning?' she echoed, and he frowned.

As far as Lucifer Mendori was concerned, she thought ruefully, the matter was at an end, other opinions did not interest him. He was already part way across the big *salon* to the door, and he turned and frowned at her impatiently. Getting to her feet Rosalind faced him, determinedly controlled despite her frantic heartbeat.

'There is some reason why you cannot be here, *signorina*?' he asked, and Rosalind did not even attempt to explain; it would, she felt, be a waste of time.

Instead she shook her head. 'Not really, *signore*,' she said. 'It's just that I was taken rather by surprise, that's all.'

Lucifer Mendori eyed her narrowly. 'I informed you that my need was immediate,' he reminded her shortly. 'I am not in the habit of repeating myself, *signorina*. I require you here by ten o'clock tomorrow morning or I shall assume that you have decided not to come at all—*capisce*?'

'Yes, of course, Signor Mendori.' She met his eyes briefly. 'I'll be here!'

'*Buono!*' He turned again, crossing the big room in long, easy strides and turning briefly in the doorway to look back at her, his black eyes gleaming. '*Addio, signorina!*'

Rosalind stood for a moment after he had gone,

gazing at the closed door and feeling slightly dizzy. For a few seconds panic took over when she realised at last the full meaning of what she had done, but it was too late to undo it now—she was committed, and Lucifer Mendori was not a man to play fast and loose with.

CHAPTER THREE

Rosalind felt terribly nervous the following morning when she set out for the Villa Mimosa, and all her previous doubts about having been too rash returned to plague her as she walked up the narrow, steep road. Signora Vincente, highly delighted at what she called her good fortune, had fussed about her as she got ready to leave, just as excited as if the venture was her own.

If the post was not resident Rosalind would of course continue to stay with her at the Villa Gardina, she insisted, but if it was then she would expect to hear all the gossip when Rosalind came to visit her. To some extent her pleasure had been infectious; it was only when Rosalind was making her solitary way to the Villa Mimosa that she became nervous and uncertain.

The question of living in was one which she preferred not to dwell on at the moment, for the thought of living under the same roof as the Mendori brothers was, she felt, enough to throw any girl into a state of nervous excitement. She had yet to meet her real employer, of course, the Contessa Mendori, but she could only hope that she would prove to be more akin to her younger grandson than the overpowering Lucifer.

When she arrived, flushed and a little breathless from the climb, she was admitted by the same manservant as before, and once again his hooded dark eyes gleamed at her appreciatively. Adolfo, Lucifer Mendori had called him, and Rosalind frankly admitted that he made her uneasy. Before they had taken more than a couple of steps across the big hall, however, a door beside the marble staircase opened and Luigi Mendori came out, hurrying across to her with his hands outstretched, as if she was some old and very dear friend.

'*Signorina!*'

His appearance startled Rosalind, but it was a welcome relief from the brooding approbation of Adolfo. Seizing her left hand he raised it to his lips while his dark eyes gleamed at her from his handsome, tanned face.

'Good morning, Signor Luigi.'

She could do nothing about the rapid beat of her heart suddenly, or the smile that came instinctively to her lips. Luigi Mendori would always make an impression, no matter where he was, but here, in this big, extravagantly decorated hall, he was as perfect a part of his environment as those bright, gilded figures depicted in the frieze.

'I am so glad that you are here,' he assured her in his deep, seductive voice. 'I was desolate not to see you yesterday!'

Rosalind was tempted to ask him why he had not asserted himself and insisted on seeing her when he was the one who had invited her to come, but having met Lucifer Mendori she could see his point of view. It would not be easy to act in defiance of his autocratic brother at any time, and the fact that he was trying to introduce into the house a strange woman whom he had met with only casually in the street would be difficult to justify.

She had no wish to discomfit him in front of Adolfo either, and the man still stood close by, waiting, although heaven knew why when Luigi obviously intended to take over. She withdrew her hand from Luigi's grasp and smiled at him, wondering why, if he was to introduce her to the Contessa Mendori, the manservant was still there.

Adolfo's presence seemed to suggest that Lucifer Mendori had given orders that he was to conduct her to the Contessa, and he probably foresaw trouble if he did not do as he was told, whether Luigi was in favour of the idea or not. The idea of annoying her new employer so soon dismayed her, but she saw little she could do about it.

'I'm to see the Contessa Mendori this morning,' she ventured, glancing briefly at Adolfo. 'She is to confirm whether or not I have the job.'

'Oh, but of course you have, *signorina*!' Luigi assured her. 'Has Lucifer not told you so?'

'He told me I have the job if the Contessa approved of me,' Rosalind said, and he smiled.

'Then it is yours, Signorina Rosalinda,' he told

45

her confidently. 'I have told her of you and how *bellissima* you are and I know she will approve of you—as I do!' His dark eyes challenged her to deny him the familiarity of her christian name and Rosalind once more found herself smiling at him. There was something irresistibly charming about Luigi Mendori that did a great deal for her self-confidence.

'I'm afraid Signor Mendori had quite the wrong idea about why I was here, Signor Luigi,' she told him. 'I had some difficulty convincing him that I was serious about working here.'

'He doubted it?' Luigi frowned. 'But why should he?'

He should have known the answer well enough, Rosalind thought ruefully, and yet his confusion sounded genuine. 'Perhaps because I'd met you only the day before,' she told him. 'It did rather give the wrong impression, *signore*. He suspected that I had—well, that I had something more than a job in mind when I came, on such short acquaintance.'

Luigi's eyes held hers steadily, neither anxious nor bold, but something between the two, and infinitely persuasive. 'And had you no other thought in mind, *signorina*?' he asked, soft-voiced. Giving her no time to answer, he raised her hand to his lips again and laughed as he shook his head. 'I hope there was also some thought for me in your wish to come here, Signorina Rosalinda,' he murmured. 'I would be most desolate if there was not!'

'Perhaps,' Rosalind admitted, 'but I am primarily interested in working here, *signore*, that is if the Contessa finds me suitable.'

'Have I not said that she will?' Luigi asked, and Rosalind pulled a wry face.

'Signor Mendori wasn't impressed by the fact that you'd recommended me without knowing anything about me,' she said, 'probably the Contessa won't be either!'

Luigi smiled confidently. 'You will see,' he told her. 'I know *la mia nonna!*' He turned and spoke to Adolfo in Italian, apparently giving him some kind of instruction, but the man glanced at Rosalind and seemed about to disagree.

'*Signore*——'

Turning on him angrily, Luigi berated him sharply in his own tongue, then enforced his instruction in English, possibly for Rosalind's benefit. 'You may leave the *signorina* with me,' he told him. 'I will take her to the Contessa!' He waved both hands at the man in dismissal. '*Andare, andare!*' He took Rosalind's arm in a firm grip. 'Come, Signorina Rosalinda,' he said, 'you will meet the most important woman in my life!'

His eyes glowed with triumph as he walked with her across the hall, leaving a glowering Adolfo standing there, and Rosalind could feel resentful dark eyes following them as they made for another door, the one that Rosalind recognised led into the *salon* she had seen yesterday. Luigi's hand still on her arm urged her forward and she swallowed hard on the churning sense of excitement she felt at meeting yet another of the strong-willed Mendoris.

It was rather like stepping back into a dream, Rosalind thought. That big cool room with its green carpet and the gilded ceiling, the gilt-framed paintings that looked down at her from the walls and reflected the same autocratic disregard for other opinions that even Luigi shared.

A lone figure occupied the big room and Rosalind caught her breath—at any moment now she would discover whether the Contessa Mendori most resembled her younger grandson or the irresistible arrogance of Lucifer. It was, she felt, an important moment to her, for she had burnt her boats when she posted that letter to England last night, resigning from her previous job.

The room was deliciously cool, although it was bright with the sunshine outside, but its size again impressed Rosalind as much as its beauty did and she wondered if she could ever get used to working in such surroundings. The high, wide windows stood open to the fragrant air from the garden and the sea, and branches of roses and mimosa wafted their scents everywhere.

There was water somewhere too, for its gentle sound reached her from outside, and little flecks of light danced on the ornate ceiling, reflected from a pool or a fountain. A soft breeze stirred long drapes at the windows and gave animation to the heads of the roses that peeped into the room around the edge of the shutters.

The woman standing beside the great marble fireplace supported herself with a silver-topped ebony stick in one hand, and she turned as they came into the room, smiling and holding out a hand to Luigi. There was a warmth in the smile, the warmth of affection, and she had eyes for no one but him at the moment.

Luigi walked across to her, taking Rosalind with him, and he bent and kissed her lightly on one cheek. '*Buon giorno, Nonna!*' he said softly. 'I missed breakfast!'

The woman scolded him softly in Italian, then looked at Rosalind and smiled, and Luigi drew her forward, his dark eyes gleaming confidently.

'*Nonna,*' he said, 'this is Signorina Rosalinda Matthews—*signorina,* my grandmother, *la* Contessa Mendori!'

Rosalind responded to the smile and accepted the proffered hand, noticing as she did so that the fingers were bent and looked painfully arthritic. Careful not to grip them too hard, she shook her hand and looked into a pair of dark eyes that were as warm and friendly as Luigi's.

The Contessa Mendori was a handsome rather than a pretty woman, and her black hair was streaked with grey, but she had a gentle, kindly manner and that, to Rosalind, was what mattered most. She was slightly taller than most of the Italian women Rosalind had seen so far, and she had the bearing that befitted her title, though none of the arrogance of her grandsons, and she recognised Rosalind's nervousness with an understanding smile.

'I am most pleased to meet you, Signorina Matthews,' she said in a slightly more exaggerated accent than Luigi's. Her free hand indicated a chair behind Rosalind. '*Prego, si accomodi!*' she said, and seated herself in one next to it while Luigi went to stand beside her, smiling across at Rosalind as bold and confident as ever.

'Thank you.' Rosalind perched herself on the very edge of the chair, and the Contessa noted the fact with an understanding smile.

'Do not be nervous, *per piacere, signorina*,' she said. 'You have nothing to fear.' The dark eyes twinkled at her mischievously, and she glanced up at Luigi, as if there was some intimate joke they shared. 'I am so glad that you did not allow Luca to frighten you away,' she told Rosalind, 'Luigi was afraid that he would.'

'Signor Mendori?' Warm colour flushed her cheeks as she shook her head and she tried to sound as if she met a challenge like Lucifer Mendori every day of her life. 'I'm not easily frightened, Contessa Mendori,' she said, 'although I found it rather an ordeal at first.' Glancing at Luigi, she hoped she managed to convey that some of the blame attached to him. 'Signor Mendori seemed to have quite the wrong idea of why I was there— until I put him right.'

'Ah!' Satisfaction gleamed in the eyes of the Contessa as she visualised her all-powerful grandson being put right, and Rosalind thought it amused her. 'You did not allow yourself to be bullied, *signorina*, that is good!'

Unwilling to give the wrong impression, Rosalind hastened to correct it. 'Oh, I'm not suggesting that Signor Mendori bullied me,' she denied. 'But in the circumstances there was bound to be a certain amount of misunderstanding.'

'Because it was Luigi who asked you to come?' the Contessa asked, and nodded her head. 'Ah *sì*, I understand, *signorina*, you were at a disadvantage.'

'I didn't realise at first,' Rosalind confessed, 'but Signor Mendori's reaction was reasonable if he thought——' She shrugged uneasily, wondering suddenly why she was bothering to excuse Lucifer Mendori's high-handed treatment of her. His family would, after all, know perfectly well what he was like—none better. 'It must have looked rather—bold, turning up at the house like that when I'd known Signor Luigi such a short time,' she said.

The Contessa was nodding her head, smiling placidly. '*Mio caro* Luca would not understand such impulsiveness,' she said. 'But you did well to make so good an impression, Signorina Matthews, when you began at such a disadvantage. Luca is now quite happy that you should be with me, therefore you must have impressed him most favourably.'

'Oh!' It was almost a shock to be told that Lucifer Mendori actually approved of her, for her own impression had been somewhat different. She was bound to admit that his grandmother was better qualified to judge his opinion, however, and the knowledge that he had been favourably impressed somehow pleased her. 'I'm glad,' she said, and again the Contessa smiled.

'You perhaps find Italian men a little—different from the English?' she suggested gently, and Rosalind glanced once more at Luigi standing beside his grandmother. Two Italian men, at least, were vastly different from anyone she had ever met before, but she was inclined to attribute their difference to their family background rather than their race.

'A little,' she admitted cautiously, and the Contessa nodded.

Looking up at Luigi, she waved a hand towards the door. 'You may leave us now, Luigi *caro*,' she told him. 'We do not need you any longer, *grazie!*'

Luigi frowned. 'But, Nonna——'

'*Se ne vada!*' the Contessa insisted, showing that she too had the Mendori arrogance when it suited her, although a smile took the edge off her dismissal. 'I wish to speak to Signorina Matthews alone, *caro*, huh?' she said. 'Are you not driving into Napoli with Luca this morning?'

'Later,' Luigi told her, looking disgruntled. 'There is plenty of time.'

'But you will leave us, *per piacere*,' the Contessa told him firmly. 'You are a—how is it you say?—a distraction, *sì*? So, you will leave me with Signorina Matthews, Luigi, and you may see her when you return from Napoli, hmm?'

'*D'accordo*,' Luigi agreed reluctantly, and came across to Rosalind. Raising her hand, he pressed it to his lips slowly, his dark eyes watching her. '*Addio*, Signorina Rosalinda,' he murmured.

As the door closed behind him the Contessa

smiled fondly and shook her head. 'Luigi is—how is it?—*incorreggibile*,' she told her, 'but he is also very charming, is he not?'

'He's very nice,' Rosalind allowed cautiously. 'Although I only met Signor Luigi the day before yesterday, Contessa, and then not again until I arrived just now.'

'Ah, but Luigi is impulsive when a woman is beautiful,' the Contessa told her. 'He was most diligent in describing you to me, *signorina*, and I am so pleased that you did not hesitate to come when he requested it.'

'I acted impulsively too,' Rosalind said. 'It's not like me at all, to simply—walk into things as I did into this, and I still can't quite believe it's happened.'

'But you have no regrets?' the Contessa asked, and Rosalind shook her head.

'None at all so far,' she said, and laughed a little unsteadily. 'It remains to be seen whether you live to regret Signor Luigi's impulsiveness in recommending me!'

'Ah no, I do not think so!' The thin, painful hands dismissed the likelihood of such a thing ever happening. 'I have trust in what Luigi tells me, *signorina*, though Luca does not.' She smiled wickedly, her dark eyes reminding Rosalind of Luigi. 'He was clever enough to ask you to come here and see me without telling Luca, thinking to make the choice for me himself, but of course——' Expressive hands betrayed long experience of Lucifer Mendori's autocratic ways, although there

53

was more resignation than resentment in the gesture.

Rosalind, wondering if the Contessa had been allowed any say in the matter at all, looked at her anxiously. 'I hope you don't feel that you're bound to accept me just because Signor Luigi suggested——' She shrugged and smiled warily. 'It seems rather an imposition to give you no say in the matter at all, and I'll understand perfectly if you want to change your mind and choose someone yourself.'

Contessa Mendori looked at her for a moment, her dark eyes thoughtful, then she reached out a hand, patted Rosalind's gently. 'You are a charming young woman, Signorina Matthews,' she told her, 'and I am content with my grandsons' choice—they have chosen well. Have no fear, I do not see anyone I have no wish to and I would have refused to even consider you if I had any doubts at all. Luigi perhaps is impulsive, but Lucifer is not, and if he has chosen you then'—she spread her hands and smiled —'I am content.'

Rosalind felt her heart fluttering, unsure just what caused such a disturbance; surely not the idea of Lucifer Mendori choosing her to work for him when obviously both his brother and his grandmother had expected him to disagree. 'I—I definitely have the job?' she asked, and the Contessa nodded.

'*Certamente, mia cara signorina!*'

'Thank you!' She felt inordinately relieved, for she wondered what on earth she would have done if the Contessa had not approved of her. 'I only hope I won't be a disappointment to you,' she said, and laughed a little lightheadedly. 'I did tell Signor Mendori that I don't speak Italian, but I do speak some French and I write it quite well. Also I've never tried being a companion before, but I'll do my best.'

'And I am sure we will have no regrets, *signorina*,' the Contessa said confidently. 'Not even Luca!' She smiled and shook her head as if that was unlikely, then went on in her charmingly accented English to explain her needs. 'I have many friends in England, France and America,' she explained, 'but I am no longer as able with my hands as I would like, and to have someone to help me with my *lettere* will be of great assistance.'

'Oh, I'm sure it will,' Rosalind agreed. 'And I'm sure I'll enjoy the change from business routine!'

She had already decided, unreservedly, that she liked the Contessa, and with her as an ally she found the prospect of being under the same roof as Lucifer Mendori a little less awesome suddenly. The Contessa's dark eyes studied her speculatively for a moment and she smiled. Resting both hands on the top of the ebony stick, she leaned forward, as if to impart a confidence.

'I shall probably be expected to share your companionship with Luigi,' she said, and laughed softly. 'You will have no objection to such an arrangement, Signorina Matthews?'

Rather stunned by the frankness of the question and the many possibilities it suggested, Rosalind hesitated for a moment before she answered. 'It rather depends, Contessa,' she said cautiously. 'If Signor Luigi asks me to go out with him any time and you have no objection, then I'll be happy to go. You're my employer, it would eventually be up to you, I imagine.'

'*No, signorina,*' the Contessa denied smilingly. 'It will be up to Luigi, and I know my grandson well—he will ask you!' She laughed and reached out to cover Rosalind's hand with one of her own. 'I am an understanding woman,' she said. 'A doting *nonna,* as Luca accuses me, perhaps, but you will not find me difficult, I think.'

'Oh, I'm sure I shan't,' Rosalind agreed, and looked round at the big, bright room. 'And this is such a beautiful house, I know I'm going to love every minute!'

'*Buono!*' The Contessa nodded her satisfaction. 'You must have Luigi show you our gardens, *signorinà,* they are very beautiful and I know he would enjoy to show them to you.'

Before Rosalind could express agreement, the door opened suddenly and Lucifer Mendori came in. With her heart thudding hard at her ribs she looked across at him and wondered, rather dazedly, if Lucifer Mendori ever simply walked into a room as other men did, or if he always made an entrance.

The room seemed to shrink with his presence, and she marvelled yet again at the sheer force of his character. One swift, raking glance confirmed not only the presence of his grandmother and Rosalind, but also the fact that they were alone, and it was obvious to Rosalind that he had expected to see his brother.

He was more casually dressed this morning, but the effect of his personality was no less stunning than it had been on first acquaintance, and she hastily sought to control her rapidly beating heart as he strode across the room towards them.

Pale grey slacks and a cream shirt threw his darkness into stark contrast and the rangy leanness of his body reminded her of a great cat—sleek and smooth, but at the same time infinitely dangerous. His firm, deep voice brought her from the realm of fantasy, edged as it was with the hint of impatience she was already familiar with.

'*Buon giorno, signorina,*' he said, and she thought how much more effective his voice sounded speaking Italian instead of his rather pedantic brand of English.

Rosalind knew she was blushing, just as surely as she knew that the Contessa had noticed it, and she tried hard to control the rate of her pulse. It was alarming the effect he could have on her. 'Good morning, Signor Mendori.'

The black eyes flicked swiftly around the room once more, and a small frown still lingered between his brows. 'I understood Luigi to be here with you, Nonna,' he told the Contessa, and she smiled and reached out a hand to him.

'As you see, he is not, *caro,*' she said. 'He brought in Miss Matthews and introduced her to me and then he left us at my request.'

'Ah!'

It was evident that Luigi's almost immediate departure satisfied him, and he again looked at Rosalind, the narrow-eyed glance missing nothing of the short blue dress she wore and the way it flattered her fairness, nor the light fawn shoes that showed off her slim ankles. She hastily crossed one leg over the other, then immediately wished she hadn't, for the full skirt of her dress was embarrassingly revealing, and she coped again with the urgent beat of her heart.

'I thought you were already gone, Luca,' the Contessa said. 'Are you taking Luigi with you this morning?'

'I am!' Lucifer agreed shortly, and his tone suggested that he was on the defensive. 'Mendori e Figli includes two sons, Nonna, and Luigi must do his share now!'

'Sì, sì, naturalmente!' the Contessa soothed, and smiled tolerantly. 'But he is not the entusiasto that you are, caro mio, you will allow for him, hmm?'

Lucifer Mendori smiled, and the effect of it in that strong satyrical face was a revelation to Rosalind. His wide mouth revealed strong even teeth and his black eyes glowed warmly as he held his grandmother's hand gently in his own large one. 'Sì, va bene,' he promised, then glanced at Rosalind sitting so uneasily in her chair. 'Is your companion to your liking, Nonna?' he asked, and the Contessa nodded.

'Sì davvero,' she said. 'I am very pleased!'

Lucifer nodded, as if satisfied. 'You will find it useful to have someone to write your letters for you, and the *signorina* is well qualified.'

'She is also a very charming *ragazza*, Luca,' the Contessa told him with a slight shake of her head. 'We will be good friends, I think.'

'*Buono!*' He turned his full attention to Rosalind and she tried her best to meet his gaze coolly and steadily, but found it harder than she would have believed. 'I believe you have left your belongings at the Villa Gardina, *signorina*,' he said. 'I will have them brought here for you, and then Teresa can show you to your room.'

'Thank you, *signore*.' Rosalind hesitated, wondering if it was inevitable that she lived in. She saw it as more or less necessary if she was to be a constant companion to the Contessa, but she had never before lived and worked under the same roof, and the thought of sharing the accommodation with Lucifer Mendori raised questions in her mind that she preferred not to face at the moment. He was a disturbing man, and unlikely to become less so on closer acquaintance. 'I wondered——' she ventured impulsively. 'I suppose it's essential that I live in, *signore*?'

His dark brows drew together ominously and Rosalind already regretted mentioning it. 'Did you not expect to live here, *signorina*?' he asked. 'Surely you cannot be of much use to the Contessa if you are living elsewhere?'

'No, I suppose not!' She glanced at the Contessa apologetically. 'I half expected to, of course, but I wasn't certain.'

Lucifer looked at her for a moment with narrowed black eyes. 'May I ask your reasons for not wishing to come here?' he asked, and Rosalind shrugged uneasily. It would be difficult enough telling any man that she was afraid of finding his presence too disturbing, with Lucifer Mendori it was impossible.

'It isn't exactly that I don't want to live here,' she admitted. 'It's simply that——'

The Contessa reached out and touched her hand. Then she looked up at her grandson, shaking her head slowly as if she rued his lack of perception. 'Luca,' she said softly, 'a young girl in a foreign country must think of her reputation. With two *vigoroso* young men in this house, the *signorina* has reason to be cautious, hmm?'

Lucifer Mendori looked at Rosalind directly for a moment or two, and she curled her hands anxiously as she bore the scrutiny, wondering what on earth was going on in his mind. 'You were less cautious when you came here alone in answer to my brother's telephone call, *signorina*,' he said quietly. 'However, I can assure you of my own good conduct. I cannot answer for my brother, he no doubt has his own reasons for wanting you here, but I have little doubt that much will depend upon your response to his advances!'

'Of course, *signore*!' Her cheeks flushed with colour, Rosalind looked at him resentfully with her chin in the air and her eyes more violet than blue between heavy lashes. He had no right to make that remark about her coming so promptly after Luigi called her, and she meant him to know how she felt. 'There was really no need to remind me how rash I was,' she told him, 'and I had no intention of making a fuss about living in, I merely wondered what was expected of me, that's all!'

'Simply that you attend to the needs of the Contessa,' he informed her coolly. 'What you do in your free time, *signorina*, is of no concern to me, as long as it does nothing to disturb the smooth running of the household.'

'I fail to see how my being here can affect the smooth running of your household!' Rosalind told him, and Lucifer looked across at her narrowly.

'You do not know my brother, *signorina*!' he retorted harshly. 'When you do you will realise just how much you could disrupt our present way of life!'

'Luca!' The Contessa's soft, reproachful voice broke across the angry silence, and Rosalind realised a little dizzily that she had very nearly become involved in a quarrel with Lucifer Mendori that could have meant the end of her new job almost before it had begun.

She looked at the Contessa and shook her head, her cheeks flushed. 'I'm sorry, Contessa,' she said in a strangely husky voice that she scarcely recognised as her own. Glancing at Lucifer Mendori from the shadow of her lashes, she allowed herself a last jibe. 'You suggested I wasn't subservient enough, Signor Mendori,' she said, 'and it seems you were right—I apologise!'

It was a ploy to get the Contessa on her side and Rosalind saw the curious frown she turned on her grandson. 'Luca,' she said, 'what does this mean?'

For a moment he said nothing, but his dark brows were drawn above glittering black eyes. 'I think the *signorina* already seeks to cause a disturbance,' he told his grandmother. 'I remarked that I thought her unsuitable for domestic service and I still consider her so!'

'But I find her most suitable for my service,' the Contessa informed him with a firmness as resolute as his own and, after a moment he inclined his head and yielded.

'*Benissimo*, Nonna,' he said quietly. 'It shall be as you wish.' He did not trouble to explain why, if he found her so unsuitable, he had agreed to employ her, but Rosalind felt a strange lightness in her heart as she sat with her hands in her lap.

CHAPTER FOUR

LIVING at the Villa Mimosa could have drawbacks, Rosalind realised. For one thing it meant her taking her meals with the family, and that proved rather disconcerting for the first couple of days until she got used to it. Occasionally their impeccable good manners gave way to instinct and the family lapsed into Italian among themselves during a meal, but whenever it happened either Luigi or the Contessa always apologised for excluding her.

Only Lucifer Mendori did nothing about it but

merely looked at her briefly with his black eyes, and apparently saw no reason to apologise. She had already decided that he was a man who would not apologise readily for anything he did. He was a law unto himself and saw no reason why he should change.

The room she had been given was much more grand than she felt she was entitled to as an employee, but presumably she fell between two stools as far as status was concerned. She was not on the same footing as the household servants, and yet she was an employee. When it came to accommodating her, however, it had evidently been decided that she should be put on the same footing as a guest or a member of the family.

Her room was big and airy and opened on to a view across the gardens at the front of the villa and the long winding drive with its guardian cypress trees. Some distance away up the steep narrow road was the motorway, invisible from there but still faintly audible, while immediately below orange and lemon trees filled her room with their familiar scent.

The décor was rather extravagantly baroque, like the rest of the villa, but it was a style she was getting used to and it certainly gave everything an air of richness. A huge gilt mirror reflected her from head to toe and glittered in the shafts of sunlight that found their way in through the shuttered windows, and an ornate gilt light fitting lent an almost ballroom grandeur when it was alight. Deep-piled rugs scattered over the crimson carpet deadened her footsteps and a crimson and gold bed-cover matched the luxury of silk drapes perfectly.

Waking in the morning made Rosalind feel that she was in reality just falling asleep and going into an extravagant dream. It was hard to believe that she would not be going back to her usual office desk in London, and she lay gazing up at the ornately carved ceiling of her bedroom with a distant hazy look in her eyes.

There was little or nothing to make her regret her impulsive move so far. She liked the Contessa, and Luigi was as charmingly attentive as she expected, even though he had not so far made the move his grandmother seemed to expect and asked her out. Only Lucifer Mendori still disturbed her far more than she cared to admit, and she thanked heaven that he was out for most of the day.

He said very little directly to her, but she was always so conscious of him whenever he was in the same room with her that she had several times wondered whether the Contessa was aware of the effect her elder grandson had on her. She hoped not, for she found it an embarrassment and fought it as hard as she could.

Hearing a whisper of movement outside on the gallery, Rosalind glanced at her wristwatch. It would be Teresa, the maid, with the Contessa's early morning coffee, she guessed, and that meant that it was time she thought about getting up herself.

Waiting for the use of a bathroom was not necessary at the Villa Mimosa, for when the villa had been modernised some years ago, each huge bedroom had merely had one end partitioned off and fitted as a bathroom, so that every bedroom had its own. It was luxurious and convenient, and the wealthy Mendoris had spared no expense to ensure their own comfort and that of their staff and guests.

Rosalind's bathroom was in black marble and white tiles, with the inevitable gilt decoration around the high ceiling, and a seemingly endless supply of hot water. She piled her long fair hair on top of her head and revelled in a long soak in scented water, listening to the sounds of a stirring household.

She took her time dressing and put on a light green dress with short sleeves and a rather low neckline, which she supposed was not really suitable wear for a secretary. But then she had not come to Crisdorfi with the intention of working as a secretary, and she had so far had little opportunity to supplement her holiday wardrobe from the shops in Naples.

More than three weeks in the Italian sun had given her fair skin a light golden tan, and her fair hair looked lighter by contrast, her eyes more deeply blue. The green dress gave her a fresh cool look that Luigi would be sure to appreciate, and she smiled at her own reflection as she took a last look in the mirror before going down to breakfast. Luigi could always be relied upon to appreciate the way she looked, even if his brother did not.

The long gallery ran almost the whole width of the villa, sweeping round at one end to accommodate other upstairs rooms, and was accessible via that grand marble staircase from the hall. Carpeted luxuriously in deep blue, it had gilded blue velvet chairs placed at intervals along its length, and alcoves in the white-painted walls that held huge vases full of roses and sweet-scented carnations, while more family portraits of past Mendoris gazed, benignly autocratic, from their gilt frames. It would take her quite some time, Rosalind decided as she left her room, to become accustomed to such luxurious surroundings.

Even breakfast was eaten in the enchanting surroundings of the gardens. On a terrace beside a pool, where tall dark cypress and lemon trees gave shade from the sun and lent their warm scent to the morning air. Rosalind had gathered from the remarks when he put in an appearance on her first day there that Luigi seldom breakfasted, and she was therefore left in the company of Lucifer Mendori and the Contessa.

She enjoyed the Contessa's company and they chatted over breakfast, gradually getting to know one another better and becoming friends in the process, so Rosalind liked to think. She found Lucifer a less easy breakfast companion, even though he said little. So far, since her arrival, he seemed to have been absorbed with the big pile of mail he had each day.

This morning as she came downstairs she could hear voices in the kitchen and recognised them as belonging to Teresa and to Maria, the cook. They sounded rather as if they were quarrelling, but

Neapolitans were excitable and garrulous people, and they could just as easily have been simply talking together as they worked.

It was warm and there was the customary air of lethargy about the beginning of the day, so that Rosalind smiled to herself. She was even beginning to accept that too, as an alternative to the early morning rush she was more used to at home. She enjoyed the light Continental breakfast and looked forward to rolls, butter and cherry jam, eaten in the coolness of the garden, so that she hurried down the last few stairs with a skip in her step.

'*Buon giorno, signorina!*'

The thickly carpeted stairs had given her no clue that anyone else was coming down behind her and Rosalind turned and looked back over her shoulder, her eyes blinking in surprise. Lucifer Mendori came swiftly down the wide staircase, as if he was attempting to catch up with her and she curled her hands instinctively as he came closer, unable to do anything about the sudden rapid beat of her heart.

'Good morning, Signor Mendori.'

There was little else she could do but wait in the hall for him, but she glanced behind him to see if there was any sign of Luigi too. She should have known it was too early for him, of course, and she faced the prospect of going in to breakfast with Lucifer, hoping that the Contessa would already be on the terrace so that she would not be thrown in to his exclusive company. That would be much too disconcerting so early in the day.

Lucifer's dark face wore a thoughtful frown

when he joined her, and Rosalind wondered what caused it—hoping it was nothing she had done. He placed a hand lightly under her arm, his touch bringing an immediate response from her unsteady pulse. 'Signorina Matthews,' he said in his customary pedantic English, 'would you not like to speak Italian?'

Rosalind took a moment to absorb the question, trying to think of the reason behind it. It was not the kind of thing she expected to be asked at that hour of the morning, especially when she was still trying to cope with the chaos he caused by curling his strong fingers in to her soft skin as they walked across the hall together.

'I—I haven't really thought about it,' she confessed. 'Is it important?'

'Not important, perhaps,' Lucifer allowed, 'but surely it would be advantageous, *signorina*.'

Rosalind glanced at him from the corners of her eyes, unsure just what lay behind his sudden interest in her education. She could see his point, of course. It would make life much simpler for them all if she spoke Italian as fluently as the Mendori family spoke English, but she did not relish taking language lessons as part of her curriculum.

'Yes, of course, I can see it might be,' she told him, 'but——'

'Then you shall learn!' he informed her in a tone that defied anyone to find reasons why she should not. 'You could begin this morning, do you not agree?'

'This morning?' Having already committed herself to a busy morning typing the Contessa's letters she did not quite see how she could fit in a tutorial session as well.

Lucifer frowned impatiently. 'All I suggest,' he told her, 'is that when you say good morning to the Contessa in a moment or two, you do so in Italian rather than in English as you did with me.'

Rosalind's head was still whirling with the sudden necessity of speaking a strange tongue when she had barely had time to gather her wits, and she felt she was being rushed into something without being given the opportunity to choose for herself. She would have liked a little more warning that she was to be confronted with the need to change to Italian, but it was, she realised, typical of Lucifer Mendori to spring something like this on her.

'I hadn't anticipated taking language lessons,' she told him, and added hastily lest he think her incapable, 'Not that I mind learning, but——'

'I am not suggesting that you take formal lessons, *signorina*,' Lucifer interrupted shortly. 'Merely that you use Italian whenever you can, learning as you go along, perhaps given a little informal coaching from day to day until you are proficient.'

'Oh, I see!' She dwelt for a moment on the prospect of his being her coach, and found it not unpleasant, as long as he did not lose patience with her.

'I'll give it a try,' she said, and Lucifer nodded, as if it was no more than he expected of her.

They continued across the hall and they were

just outside the door leading into the *salon* when he brought her to a halt, his fingers tight on her arm as he turned her to face him. 'You would perhaps like to try saying good morning before you go in, and surprise the Contessa?' he suggested, and Rosalind blinked, taken by surprise yet again. 'You know what it is?' he asked, obviously containing his patience with difficulty.

He was notoriously impatient, and it was that that made her hesitant about accepting his idea. 'I'm not sure,' she told him, giving herself time to think. 'I think so.'

'*Buon giorno,*' he said carefully, his black eyes fixed on her mouth in a way that was infinitely disturbing. 'You can say *buon giorno*, can you not, *signorina?*'

'Oh, yes, I expect so!'

'Try!' The brief command brooked no argument.

'Now?' Rosalind looked up at him and saw resignation as well as the inevitable impatience.

'Now!' he said firmly. 'Come, *signorina*, it is not so difficult, surely! You are an intelligent woman and not as obtuse as you would have me believe, I think!'

'Don't rush me!' Rosalind told him, hasty in her own defence. 'I didn't anticipate having to learn Italian before I've even had my breakfast!'

Briefly a glint of amusement showed in the black eyes that looked down at her, and he shook his head. 'You are under no obligation, *signorina*,' he told her quietly, 'but the Contessa would be pleased if you made the attempt.' He arched a brow and again she caught a glimmer of amusement, of warmth, in his eyes. 'You think me a bully, am I not right?' he asked, and the deep, warm sound of his laughter was unexpected enough to startle her.

'No,' she said, as steadily as her racing pulses allowed. 'No, of course I don't think you're a bully, Signor Mendori.'

'No?'

The invitation to comment was irresistible and Rosalind looked at him straight for a moment. 'You're used to having your own way and to having your every wish obeyed,' she told him with a breathless bravado, 'but you aren't really a bully!'

'You flatter me, *signorina*!' For a moment his eyes glittered as if he resented her frankness, but then he inclined his head briefly and the strong fingers about her arm held her firmly facing him. 'Then you will try saying *buon giorno* instead of good morning, hmm?' he asked.

Rosalind felt rather self-conscious and hated the thought of making a fool of herself if at any minute either Teresa or Maria came through the door from the kitchen and witnessed her impromptu Italian lesson. But after hastily glancing over her shoulder, she did as he said, forming the words self-consciously and refusing to look at him while she did so.

'*Buon giorno*,' she said, and glanced up hastily when she realised he was shaking his head.

'*No, no!*' He used his bunched fingers to show

her the shape he wanted, then spanned her chin with one large hand and gently but firmly squeezed her cheeks, pursing her mouth into the necessary pout. Rosalind thought her heart would stop, it was beating so hard, for the way he held her face up to him suggested that he was about to kiss her, and the anticipation was breathtaking. 'The lips, *signorina*,' he said. 'You do not purse the lips enough! So!'

'*Buon giorno.*' She repeated the phrase again with his fingers persuading her mouth into the correct pronunciation, and this time he nodded approvingly.

'*Migliore!*' he said. 'That is better!'

Rosalind struggled with the effect of his being so close, and wondered a little dazedly why she should feel so inordinately pleased that he had praised her accent. The strong fingers now merely rested lightly on her cheeks with the merest suggestion of movement in their tips, caressing her soft skin. She was blushing like a schoolgirl and suddenly felt so vulnerable that she despaired of her own weakness. He had the ability to arouse her as no man ever had before, and she hated the sense of helplessness it gave her, so that her reaction was instinctively defensive.

'*Grazie, signore!*' she said, sounding disturbingly breathless. 'I'm flattered you approve!'

It was a mistake to have been sarcastic, she realised that as soon as the words left her mouth, but it was too late now. The warmth was gone from his black eyes as they searched her face and the touch of his hand on her face was without any suggestion of a caress. Her heart had a rapid and urgent beat when he released her suddenly and bobbed his dark head in a stiff little mock bow.

'I apologise, *signorina*,' he said, an edge of steel on his voice. 'I should have remembered that you do not like to be instructed!'

Rosalind shook her head hastily. She already regretted that impulsive and sarcastic retort, but he would not be interested in her reasons or her apologies now. She had snubbed his efforts to help her and he would resent it bitterly, as only a man like him could who had allowed himself to soften and been mocked for his efforts.

'I don't mind learning Italian at all,' she told him, trying to vindicate herself to some extent. 'I'd like to learn, but——'

'You would, of course, prefer that my brother instruct you—I understand perfectly, *signorina*!' The hard, glittering expression in his eyes showed that he would not easily be appeased, and she regretted that more than she dared admit. 'No doubt you will arrange something with Luigi,' he said. 'In a manner more to your liking!'

It was difficult for Rosalind to believe, but he seemed to actually resent the idea of Luigi helping her, and she could not control the little thrill of pleasure it gave her. The idea of Lucifer Mendori wanting to help her learn Italian opened up all sorts of interesting possibilities, and she despaired of her own rashness in spoiling the opportunity.

'I didn't *say* I wanted to learn from Luigi!' she said. 'I never even thought about it!' She caught the look in his eyes as he gazed down at her—a deep, unfathomable look that made her shiver suddenly. 'I don't think he'd make a very good teacher,' she ventured, and Lucifer's wide mouth twitched briefly into the ghost of a smile.

'I am glad there is one point on which we agree, *signorina*,' he said quietly. 'Luigi would not have the necessary ability to concentrate in such circumstances!'

'And you would, of course!' Roslind retorted, rashly impulsive.

Lucifer looked at her narrowly for several seconds, and his black eyes were glittering like jet in that satyr-like face. Then a hint of smile once more touched his wide mouth and he inclined his head slightly in a mock bow. 'You do yourself an injustice, *signorina*,' he said, 'and you also credit me with less human qualities than I possess!'

Her heart thudding heavily in her breast, Rosalind hastily avoided his eyes. In the circumstances her remark must have sounded quite provocative, and the wonder was that he was apparently more amused than angry about it. 'I wasn't making any sort of implication at all,' she told him in a husky voice. 'I shouldn't have been so hasty, Signor Mendori—I'm sorry.'

'Are you?' Something in his voice made her glance up quickly and in the same moment he reached out for her, his hands on her upper arms, drawing her to him irresistibly. There was no time to say or do anything before his mouth covered hers, firm and hard and incredibly sensual but without passion or anger. He released her slowly, his mouth lingering lightly on hers, then he let her go suddenly and looked down at her with glittering black eyes. 'Shall we go in?' he asked quietly.

He opened the door of the *salon*, then stood aside for her to precede him and Rosalind brushed past him quickly, instinctively catching her breath when her bare arm briefly touched the warmth of his hand. Her heart was beating so hard that she felt lightheaded as she crossed the big room to the sunny terrace beyond.

She thanked heaven that the Contessa was already sitting at the round white table in the shade of the cypress trees, for she could not face having breakfast alone with Lucifer at the moment, and it was much too early for Luigi to put in an appearance.

The Contessa looked up and smiled when she saw them, holding out a welcoming hand to Lucifer, who went straight to her. Bending his dark head he kissed her, murmuring his greeting in Italian, then he looked directly across at Rosalind as she sat down and arched one brow quizzically.

'*Signorina?*' he prompted, and Rosalind glanced at him briefly before addressing the Contessa.

'*Buon giorno*, Contessa,' she said, and quickly recalled another phrase Luigi had taught her. '*Comé sta?*'

The Contessa smiled and a glint of amusement showed in Lucifer's eyes as he sat himself next to her at the table. '*Buon giorno, mia cara,*' the Contessa said. '*Sto molto bene, grazie.* You are going to speak in Italian?' she asked, and Rosalind too glanced across at Lucifer before she answered.

'I'm going to try,' she said. 'Signor Mendori thinks it might be a good idea and I'd like to learn.' She laughed a little uncertainly, and again glanced briefly at Lucifer. 'Whether it works or not remains to be seen,' she said.

It was obvious that the Contessa was in favour of the idea and she nodded encouragingly. 'But why should it not?' she asked. 'You will soon learn, *mia cara signorina,* when you have been with us for some time. Unless you are considering lessons,' she added, and her dark eyes studied Rosalind for a few moments thoughtfully. 'Luigi would enjoy to be your *maestro,* I am sure, Signorina Matthews, huh?'

Lucifer was watching her, Rosalind was aware of it, and she studiously avoided looking at him. He had poured himself coffee and sat drinking it slowly, the cup held in both hands, confident and at ease as he waited for her to make her decision. 'I don't know yet, Contessa,' she said. 'Nothing's been decided. Luigi doesn't even know about it yet.'

'Ah!' Contessa Mendori looked swiftly from one to the other, her fine brows arched curiously, and her gaze finally came to rest on Lucifer's dark, inscrutable face. '*You* would instruct *la signorina,* Luca *caro?*' she asked softly, and Lucifer shrugged his broad shoulders casually as he set down his coffee cup.

'*Non so*, Nonna,' he said quietly. 'We will see.'

It was inevitable that before very long Luigi would issue the invitation that his grandmother had anticipated, but Rosalind had been at the Villa Mimosa for almost three weeks when he asked her if she would like to drive into Naples with him after lunch one day. She hesitated only because she wondered if he should perhaps have been at the works, and whether Lucifer would see her as yet another excuse for his brother to evade his responsibilities.

They were walking in the gardens and Luigi, bronzed and handsome in light trousers and a white shirt, was looking at her in such a way that it would be very hard to refuse him anything. He had already established the ruling that she call him Luigi instead of his more formal title, and he in turn called her Rosalinda, preferring the Italian version of her name. Partly, she guessed, because it sounded more romantic.

He held her hand lightly in his as they passed under the shade of the cypress trees beside the pool, and the pressure of his fingers on hers was just enough to suggest that other, more exciting pleasures were on his mind. His dark eyes beamed down at her as she hesitated to give him a direct answer, but she knew from his air of confidence that he had no doubt at all she would do as he wanted eventually.

'Will you not come with me, *bella* Rosalinda?' he insisted persuasively, and Rosalind shook back her hair from her face, smiling at his blatant tactics but finding them irresistible all the same.

'I'd like to, of course,' she told him, 'but I can't help wondering if your brother expects you to be at the works with him, Luigi.'

He shrugged carelessly, but it was obvious that he found the subject distasteful. 'Who cares what Lucifer thinks?' he asked, and Rosalind pulled a face, laughing and shaking her head.

'I have to,' she told him. 'To all intents Signor Mendori is my employer and if he thinks I'm encouraging you to stay away from the works, I might well find myself out of a job.'

'Oh, he will not do that without angering Nonna,' Luigi assured her confidently, 'and he does not like to do anything to upset Nonna. Also he does not expect me to attend the *ufficio* each day as he does.'

'But shouldn't you?' Rosalind insisted. 'Go in every day, I mean—Signor Mendori seems to think you should.'

'Hah!' The dramatic gesture he made with his free hand was both despairing and resigned and it dismissed his brother's passion for business affairs as beyond his comprehension. 'Lucifer does not mind giving up his whole life to Mendori e Figli, but I do!'

'He works very hard at it,' Rosalind said. 'But I suppose he has to to make it a success.'

'Perhaps.' He shrugged as if his brother's devotion to his work made him uneasy, perhaps it even troubled his conscience, Rosalind thought.

'Ever since our grandfather died Lucifer is the one who makes everything work,' Luigi said, 'but soon he will lose it all if he is not careful.'

'Lose it?' Rosalind made no pretence of lack of interest and the idea of Lucifer losing everything he worked so hard for stunned her for a moment. 'But how could he lose it?'

Luigi shrugged, but his hand held hers just a little more tightly, she thought. 'It is not yet his, you understand,' he told her. 'Oh, Lucifer is—how do you say?—the head man to all appearances, but Nonna is still the owner of Mendori e Figli until he becomes *trentacinque*—thirty-five—years old.'

Which, thought Rosalind a little dazedly, could not be so long now, for he was some years older than Luigi, she guessed, and Luigi was in his late twenties. 'He has to wait until then before he actually takes over?' she asked, and Luigi nodded.

'And then only if he is married.'

Rosalind stared at him for a moment, but there was no indication that Luigi was teasing her and she shook her head, frowning curiously. 'Do you mean to say that he loses it all if he doesn't marry?' she asked.

'*Sì*—Nonno Mendori believed that a man should be married and have a family.'

In fact it had crossed Rosalind's mind more than once why a man as attractive as Lucifer Mendori was not married, and in view of the conditions of inheritance it was even more surprising. It also seemed rather unfair, she thought. 'So there are conditions,' she said, and Luigi nodded.

'If Lucifer is not married by the age of thirty-five when he should inherit the business, then he loses it all and it will come to me when I too am thirty-five years old and married.'

'And you think you *will* be married by then?' Rosalind asked.

He nodded, his voice matter-of-fact. '*Naturalmente*,' he said. 'But I shall choose carefully—a wife who will allow me to inherit Mendori e Figli and who will also—how is it?—turn the blind eye, hmm?' He laughed and shook his head, as if his brother's reticence in the matter of acquiring a bride was beyond his understanding. 'Lucifer is foolish to risk so much when it is so easy to find a wife—I would not take such a chance!'

Luigi's sheer practicality on the matter of marriage was not entirely a surprise, but what intrigued Rosalind most at the moment was why Lucifer would put his whole future in jeopardy by staying single. It was not like him, she felt, to fail to provide for anything so important, unless he had a very good reason.

She reached out with her free hand and pulled a white rose from its branch, holding it close to her nose to inhale its perfume for a moment. With Luigi she walked slowly around the edge of the pool, two contrasting figures amid the profusion of flowers and trees, the air heady with the scent of lemons and roses. Rosalind's fair head reached only to just above Luigi's shoulder and she did not look up at him when she spoke because she did not want him to know just how much his brother's affairs interested her. The depth of her interest surprised even her, but she made no effort to wonder why.

'Surely Lucifer must have had plenty of opportunities to marry,' she ventured, hoping she sounded sufficiently casual. 'He's a very attractive man.'

'And many women would be willing to marry him,' Luigi said, pulling a face. 'He has not a dislike of women, you understand,' he stressed, 'but being Lucifer he will not marry simply for the sake of gaining Mendori e Figli—he must find just the woman he wants!'

'Wants?' The choice of words startled her until she realised it was merely Luigi's way of wording it.

He shrugged casually, almost reluctant to admit it, it seemed. 'A woman he loves,' he said, and Rosalind twirled the white rose slowly between her fingers, looking down at it with its scented head already drooping in the warm sun.

Her heart beat slightly faster as she put her question, still without looking at him. 'And he's never found her yet?' she asked.

Luigi shrugged. 'One supposes not,' he said, 'but it is not surprising, Rosalinda, when he has spent so many years devoting his whole time to Mendori e Figli and making us even more wealthy than we were when Nonno Mendori was in charge!'

'And now he stands a chance of losing it all,' Rosalind said, half to herself. 'It hardly seems fair, Luigi.'

'Maybe not, *bella mia*,' Luigi agreed, 'but he has

yet to find the woman he wants.' He laughed shortly and shook his head. '*Dio mio!*' he said with a flash of impatience. 'I would not risk so much for the sake of finding the right woman!'

Which was probably no more than the truth, Rosalind thought, but could not resist a smile for Luigi's strictly practical view of love and marriage. It was ironic in one way that the situation should be as it was. Luigi, generally reckoned to be the romantic one, was prepared to marry almost any suitable female to ensure his inheritance, while Lucifer, the apparently businesslike one of the brothers, remained single and risked losing everything, simply because he would marry only the woman he felt was right for him.

'How long is there for him—I mean, how long does he have to find a wife?' Rosalind asked, and Luigi looked down at her for a moment, then laughed and squeezed her fingers tightly.

Bending his dark head, he brushed a light, teasing kiss on her cheek. 'Why, *cara mia?*' he asked softly. 'Are you thinking that perhaps you will apply for the post of Lucifer's wife too?'

Rosalind felt the colour flood warmly into her cheeks, even though she hastened to deny that any such thought was in her mind. 'That's one job for which Signor Mendori would turn me down flat!' she told him, her voice curiously husky, and again Luigi laughed as he put his arm about her shoulders and hugged her close, planting a kiss on her brow.

'I might consider you for the post of my wife,

bella mia, huh?' He laughed delightedly and hugged her again, ignoring or not noticing the reproachful look she gave him from the corners of her eyes. 'Also,' he went on in a more thoughtful vein, '*la mia nonna* is making the—what you call—all-out effort to find Lucifer a wife before ten months' time when he becomes thirty-five.'

Rosalind leaned back against the arm that encircled her shoulders and looked up at him curiously, a steady, hard beat thudding away in her breast as she thought over his words and wondered just how serious he was. 'Do you mean the Contessa's going—going to find him a wife?' she asked, not quite believing it, although there was no sign of mischief on Luigi's good-looking face.

'She will try,' he assured her solemnly. 'Nonna may seem to you to be in my favour, Rosalinda, but she is also a good business woman and she knows that Mendori e Figli will prosper more in the hands of Lucifer than in mine. She means to find him a wife before it is too late.'

Still finding it very hard to believe, Rosalind shook her head. There was a lot against Lucifer Mendori accepting his grandmother's choice of a wife for him, she thought, and yet surely Luigi knew his brother better than she did herself. She looked at him curiously. 'I can't believe that Lucifer—your brother would simply marry someone his grandmother—or anyone else—had picked out for him,' she said. 'He doesn't strike me as that kind of a man, Luigi, and if he's remained single all this time because he hasn't yet found the

83

woman he—wants, then——'

'Then Nonna will make sure that he has plenty to choose from,' Luigi said confidently, and laughed, shaking his head over her solemn face. 'It will be much fun, *cara*, will it not? Seeing Lucifer's prospective brides paraded before him until he becomes so *disperato* that he will choose one for the sake of peace. Nonna Mendori is a very determined woman, Rosalinda *cara*!'

'And I'd say that Lucifer Mendori was a very determined man!' Rosalind declared.

Luigi laughed, brushing his cheek against hers and kissing her forehead lightly, his voice muffled against her hair. 'We shall see who is the more determined, eh, *cara mia*?' he said.

CHAPTER FIVE

LUIGI'S remarks about his grandmother finding Lucifer a wife appeared to be well founded, Rosalind thought, judging by the activities of the next week or so. The Contessa had sent out invitations to friends asking them if they would like to come and spend some time at the Villa Mimosa during the summer months, and each invitation, Rosalind noticed, included a daughter or, as in one case, a niece.

It was possible that some of the ladies invited had an inkling of what lay behind the invitations, and she wondered if any of them were likely to refuse. On second thoughts, she decided, it was unlikely that many people would object to having one of the wealthy Mendoris for a son-in-law.

Rosalind found it hard at first to attribute such calculated determination to the Contessa's apparently gentle nature, but the more she got to know her, the more she was forced to recognise just how much more closely Lucifer resembled his grandmother than Luigi did.

Lucifer would let little or nothing deter him from his chosen path in no matter what direction, but his grandmother was equally determined. She had set her mind on finding him a suitable wife, with or without his knowledge or approval, and she would go through with her plans with as much drive as he would have done to achieve his own ends.

Rosalind could only assume that he must either be oblivious of the plans afoot for him, or else he chose to ignore them, for he showed no sign of curiosity or irritation concerning the number of guests who were being invited to the villa, or about the fact that in each case the invitation included a young and unattached female.

But for all the Contessa's seeming confidence in her well-laid plans for choosing a bride for him, Rosalind still had little doubt about who was the stronger and more determined character of the two. In fact it gave her quite a thrill of satisfaction to think of Lucifer digging in his heels when it came to the point.

Two more invitations lay on top of the letters just signed by the Contessa, and Rosalind paused to speculate on Luigi's reaction to having the house filled with a progression of nubile young women. He might even find himself a bride from among his grandmother's friends, although Rosalind thought it unlikely he would go that far. Luigi would more likely wait until his inheritance was in danger before he took such a drastic step—he was far too fond of his freedom.

'We will have a *festa*—how do you say?—a party,' the Contessa said, looking intensely pleased with herself. 'We will have many parties, Rosalinda, huh?'

'It'll be nice while your friends are here,' Rosalind agreed, but could not help wondering what Lucifer's reaction would be to a round of parties disturbing his peace.

'It will be good!' the Contessa said confidently, and smiled her satisfaction, her dark eyes gleaming. 'It will do good for everyone to bring *la dolce vita* to this old house, I think. It is so long since I saw my friends, and friends should see each other often, do you not agree, Rosalinda?'

'Oh, yes, of course, when it's possible,' Rosalind agreed with a smile.

The Contessa picked up the two invitations from the top of the pile of letters, neatly handwritten and with her own large, scrawling signature across the bottom, and handed them to Rosalind to put into their envelopes. She had disliked the idea of sending typewritten letters to her more intimate friends, so Rosalind had taken them down in long-hand at her dictation, adding a footnote to each one, explaining why they could not be written personally.

Three had been despatched during the past week, and these latest ones made five altogether. There were two to America, two to France and one, a little surprisingly, to Rome which was little more than two hundred kilometres along the coast. It was plain that the Contessa favoured the Italian girl, possibly because she could more easily be invited back to the villa should Lucifer show any sign of liking her.

It was difficult suddenly, standing with the two invitations in her hand, not to show how she felt about the whole idea of organising people into a marriage. It did nothing to help either when she realised that it was because Lucifer Mendori was concerned that she disliked the whole thing so vehemently.

Luigi, on his own confession, was quite willing to marry for the sake of inheriting the Mendori company, and Rosalind had no doubt he meant it. Lucifer, on the other hand, had less mercenary views when it came to choosing a wife, if his brother was to be believed, and it was perhaps this reputedly uncharacteristic streak of romanticism in his otherwise ruthless character that attracted her so much. It made her hate the idea of his being manoeuvred into changing his principles for the sake of the company.

'You like parties, *cara mia*?' The Contessa's

gently enquiring voice brought her back to earth again, and Rosalind nodded hastily.

'Oh, yes, Contessa,' she said. 'As a matter of fact I went to a birthday party the evening before I left for Italy.'

The Contessa was looking at her curiously, as if she found her former air of preoccupation rather puzzling. 'Your own birthday, perhaps?' she suggested, but Rosalind shook her head.

'No, Contessa,' she said. 'It was an old school friend—someone I've kept in touch with.'

The Contessa still looked at her thoughtfully. 'A boy-friend?' she asked, and Rosalind shook her head.

'No, a girl.'

'Ah!' The Contessa nodded. There was a warm, gentle look in her eyes that belied her businesslike planning of Lucifer's future so that Rosalind found it difficult for a moment to reconcile the two such different aspects of the old lady's character. 'You are very young to be away from your home and living in a strange land,' she remarked. 'Are your family not concerned for you?'

Rosalind smiled and shook her head. 'They know I'm level-headed enough to know what I'm doing, Contessa,' she assured her. 'Lots of girls live and work abroad these days, and some of them are younger than I am.'

Contessa Mendori looked as if she found such a thing hard to believe. 'If I had a daughter I would not have let her go so far away,' she said firmly. 'Not until she had a *marito* to take care of her!'

She smiled curiously, tilting her head to one side as she spoke. 'Tell me, *bambina*, how old are you?'

'I'll be twenty-four on my next birthday,' Rosalind told her, and the Contessa shook her head over her own curiosity.

'And I am not discreet to ask such a question,' she suggested, a self-criticism that Rosalind hastened to deny.

'I don't mind in the least,' she said. 'I'm not old enough to mind being asked, Contessa, but I'm too old for you to think of me as a child!' She laughed and shook back the long fair hair from her face. 'I recognise the word *bambina*,' she told her, 'even though Signor Mendori despairs of my progress in Italian!'

Contessa Mendori shook her head, a small frown drawing her finely arched brows together for a moment. She looked at Rosalind's face with a disconcerting steadiness so that Rosalind wondered if she had been unwise to complain of Lucifer's criticism. 'I have noticed, Rosalinda,' the Contessa said, 'that Lucifer seems to consider it his right to correct your pronunciation when you speak Italian. You must not mind his authority, *bambina*—I have told him that Luigi will correct you where it is necessary; he does not take such things upon himself without your request to do so!'

'Oh, but I really don't mind at all!' Rosalind assured her anxiously. The last thing she wanted was for the Contessa to reprimand Lucifer for helping her and she hoped it had not happened too often already.

'He is an impatient man,' the Contessa went on, ignoring her defence of Lucifer, 'and he does not always understand that everyone is not so quick to learn as he is himself.'

'But I really don't mind,' Rosalind insisted. 'It was his idea that I learned to speak Italian and he offered to help me himself; it was only because——' She shrugged uneasily without finishing her explanation, and the Contessa was looking at her curiously.

'You preferred that Luigi teach you?' she suggested, and Rosalind denied it almost without stopping to think.

'He *thought* I preferred it!' she said.

The Contessa said nothing for a moment, but it was plain that she could not quite understand the whole situation and she finally shrugged her elegant shoulders in a gesture that was reminiscent of Luigi. 'It is of no matter,' she decided. 'Luca will do as he pleases with or without your consent—he is his own law!'

In view of the plotting going on behind his back, Rosalind thought Lucifer was going to need all his strength of will in a short time from now, and she once more looked at the neatly written invitations she held in her hand. 'I'm grateful for his help,' she said. 'He gets very little free time from the business, does he?'

'*Vero poco*,' the Contessa agreed quietly. 'Without Luca the business would die. Luigi——' She smiled and shook her head. 'Ah, *mio caro* Luigi, he is so much like his poor papa, my only son. Luigi loves life, he is a Mendori! Luca is so much more strong and I have no wish to see Mendori e Figli in the hands of anyone else, not even Luigi!' She shook her head slowly, and Rosalind thought she was no longer with her in spirit, but contemplating the future as well as the past. Perhaps speculating on the possible effect on the business if Lucifer did not marry, as he must to inherit. 'I am an old woman, Rosalinda,' she said, 'and I shall be thankful when Luca has control. The time will not be long now, *Dio grazie!*'

With the knowledge she had, Rosalind found it hard to feign ignorance, but she had no way of knowing what the Contessa's reaction would be to a stranger knowing so much about her family's affairs. Needing to find an answer she decided on a compromise. 'Luigi mentioned that Signor Mendori inherits the business when he's thirty-five,' she ventured, and the Contessa nodded, apparently not in the least disturbed that she knew.

'If all goes well,' she agreed. 'There is much to be done before that happens!' She looked at Rosalind curiously. 'You know also that Lucifer must marry before he can inherit?'

Rosalind nodded. There was no point in denying that she knew when Luigi had probably told her anyway. 'Luigi told me,' she said, and the Contessa nodded, as if it was no more than she expected.

'My late husband, Conte Pietro Mendori, meant to provide for a male heir to the title and the business,' she explained in the same quiet, gentle voice.

'Ourselves we had only one son, Benito, the father of Lucifer and Luigi, and he was killed so tragically soon. Pietro made the rule that whoever inherited must have a wife and, if possible, *bambini*.' She pulled a wry face over Lucifer's lack of co-operation in that direction. 'How could he know that Luca would have this—how is it you say?'

'Sentimental streak?' Rosalind suggested impulsively, and immediately felt guilty for implying that it was a weakness.

The Contessa was looking at her curiously. 'Ah!' she said. 'So you also know how it is with Lucifer, *mia cara*, hmm?'

Rosalind hastened to explain, a warm flush colouring her cheeks. 'Luigi simply said that Lucifer wouldn't marry just to inherit the business,' she said.

The Contessa's dark eyes still watched her, slightly narrowed, as if she suspected criticism. 'And you approve of such sentiments, *bambina*?' she asked.

Looking down at the letters in her hand, Rosalind hesitated, then nodded her head. 'I—I sympathise with them,' she confessed, and the Contessa was nodding her head.

Reaching out with one gnarled hand, she touched her fingers lightly. 'It is a romantic view which Luca cannot afford to indulge, *piccola*,' she told her. 'So much depends upon him that he should not hesitate to do what is required of him and find a wife.' She looked at her with a wicked gleam in her dark eyes. 'Luigi has told you of my plan for *mio ostinato* Luca, huh?' she asked, and Rosalind nodded uneasily, not at all happy about discussing the subject.

She could hardly tell the Contessa that she disapproved of her matchmaking, but she felt she might be tempted if she was drawn into discussing it. She glanced down again at the invitations in her hand and nodded. 'I know that you hope to—to find someone that Signor Mendori will like well enough to—to marry her,' she said, finding it incredibly hard to put into words.

Something in her voice must have betrayed how she felt for all the effort she made to control it, for the Contessa was looking up at her with one elegant brow raised in question. 'And you think me a scheming *femmina,* not so?' She smilingly shook her head before Rosalind could reply. 'Well, perhaps I am so, *cara,*' she admitted, 'but I know what is best for Mendori e Figli, and Lucifer must have a wife. I have said nothing of his refusing to use the title which his family have borne so proudly for so long, but in this I am adamant!'

The title—Rosalind blinked, recalling the Contessa's reference to her late husband, and she realised that now, with her son dead, her eldest grandson must also have inherited the title. 'He doesn't use the title?' she said, and the Contessa shrugged. It was obvious it displeased her, but it was something she was resigned to.

'He tells me it is—how do you say?—outmoded,' she said indignantly, 'so he prefers to be Signor Mendori! Phss!' She made an impatient sound with her pursed lips, her dark eyes flashing. 'We will see whether his wife is content to be a *signora* of if she will insist on her title of Contessa!'

Brought back reluctantly once more to the subject of Lucifer's bride, Rosalind shook her head. It was difficult not to state her own views frankly and bluntly, but discretion was best in the present circumstances, and she really liked the old lady despite her ruthless determination to have Lucifer married off.

'Do—do you really think he'll choose one of the ladies you've invited here, Contessa?' she asked, and the Contessa smiled.

'I am hopeful, *bambina*,' she said quietly. 'I am very hopeful, for much depends upon it!'

It would be another three weeks before the first of the Contessa's visitors arrived, so that there was plenty of time to make preparations, and it was no real surprise, to Rosalind at least, to discover that the Italian family from Rome were due to arrive first. Although she thoroughly disliked the whole situation, Rosalind could not help feeling a certain curiosity regarding Signorina Giovanna Cassini, and she more than once toyed with the idea of asking Luigi if he knew her and knew what she looked like. Only a natural reticence and Luigi's possible reaction to her curiosity deterred her.

It appeared that Lucifer was still unaware of the real reason for the expected influx of his grandmother's friends, and during the ensuing weeks, since the invitations had been sent out, Luigi had more than once speculated on his brother's reaction when he knew what was in store for him.

It was foolish in the extreme, she supposed, to think of Lucifer Mendori as the innocent victim in a plot to marry him off, but the feeling somehow persisted, and she wished she had the nerve to let drop to him just a hint of what the Contessa had in mind. It was difficult to believe he didn't know what was going on, and yet his composure was as unruffled as ever.

She glanced at him now across the lunch table, concealing her interest with the thickness of her lashes and wondering yet again just what he would do if he knew. The instinct to warn him both puzzled and disturbed her, for she knew he would treat her concern with scorn if he did indeed know already and simply chose to ignore the matter until it suited him to voice his opinion.

Even after weeks of living under his roof, Rosalind could still find new and unexpected facets to his character, although his strong, aggressive personality made nonsense of her present view of him. Lucifer Mendori was the last man to be cast in the role of innocence, in any shape or form.

It only occurred to her that she was still looking at him when he raised his head suddenly and caught her eye, and by then it was too late to look away. 'Did I understand you to say that you wish to visit Napoli this afternoon, *signorina*?' he asked, and Rosalind nodded.

'That's right,' she agreed, glancing briefly at Luigi. 'I didn't know if——'

'Then perhaps I may be permitted to drive you?' Lucifer suggested, making it not so much a question as an already settled fact, and Rosalind stared at him for a moment, too dazed by the unexpectedness of it to answer.

Surprise was not hers alone either, for both Luigi and the Contessa were looking at him curiously. The Contessa said nothing, but Luigi was quick to object, and he frowned at his brother darkly. 'I insist upon taking you myself, Rosalinda,' he told her. 'You would rather come with me, huh?'

He looked as if he had absolutely no doubt about it, but Rosalind glanced hastily from one to the other, uncertain what to do. She could hardly believe that Lucifer had actually offered to drive her into Naples, and yet she had heard him plainly enough and so had the other two. What his reason was, she was not yet sure, but no doubt he would have a good and practical one.

Luigi had that appealing, irresistible look in his dark eyes that she always found so hard to refuse, but Lucifer's black gaze was once more concentrating on his meal and his voice was quietly matter-of-fact as he answered his brother before Rosalind had a chance to do so.

'You have an appointment to see Signor Caccino this afternoon, Luigi,' he reminded him. 'Had you forgotten?'

'I have not forgotten,' Luigi told him, although it was obvious that he did not like being reminded. Luigi hated business appointments and made no secret of it.

'Then how are you in a position to escort Signorina Matthews?' Lucifer asked, relentlessly pressing home the point. 'The *signorina* is not familiar with Napoli.' He glanced across at Rosalind and raised a brow. 'Is that not so, *signorina?*' She nodded silently, and he turned again to his brother. 'Would you merely deposit her at some street corner and leave her to find her own way while you went on to join Signor Caccino?' he demanded, knowing the answer well enough.

'*Naturalmente no!*' Luigi denied, and Lucifer raised one black brow.

'Ah! Then how would you arrange things, huh?'

Luigi looked uneasy, and a little sulky, glancing at his grandmother for support that was not forthcoming in this instance. All of them knew well enough how Luigi would have arranged it, but he hated to have to admit it. 'I would not see Caccino,' he said, reluctantly honest, and Lucifer nodded, as if it was exactly as he expected.

'Twice during the last month you have made appointments with important men who work for us, Luigi,' he reminded him, 'and on both occasions you have failed to make an appearance.' His black eyes gleamed determinedly and there was a suggestion of tightness about his mouth that Luigi noticed uneasily. 'I realise, of course,' Lucifer went on quietly, 'that gallantry has made you put the convenience of a lady before a business appointment, no matter how important, that is why in this instance I anticipated that the *signorina*'s wish to visit Napoli would again put you in a predicament. This time, however, you need not concern yourself with the *signorina*'s safety—I will escort her while you keep your appointment with Signor Caccino! *Capisce?*'

For a moment it looked as if Luigi might argue the matter, but discretion prevailed and he merely shrugged a little sulkily. Rosalind felt herself the unwitting cause of the friction between them, something she regretted deeply, but at the same time she could not deny a flutter of excitement at the thought of being escorted by Lucifer Mendori, no matter what his reasons were, for taking her.

He had neatly forestalled his brother's truancy by taking away his excuse, but she could not help feeling a certain sympathy with Luigi at being so coolly out-manoeuvred. Looking across at him, she smiled. 'Of course you couldn't break an appointment to take me out, Luigi,' she said, 'I wouldn't dream of asking you to.' She glanced at Lucifer from the corners of her eyes, making the explanation as much for his benefit as Luigi's. 'If I'd realised you were breaking business appointments to take me out, I wouldn't have come with you, you must know that.'

'I knew it,' Luigi admitted, and looked across at her hopefully. 'Tomorrow I also have to see someone about the business,' he told her, 'but after that——'

Rosalind shook her head, feeling rather mean but unable to resist the opportunity Lucifer presented her with. 'I've rather set my heart on going today,' she told him. 'It's my free afternoon and as Signor Mendori's offered to take me——'

'You will go with him?' Luigi asked, clearly not in favour of the idea, and Rosalind glanced once more at Lucifer before she replied.

'Yes, of course,' she said. 'Why shouldn't I?'

Luigi's dark, resentful eyes flicked briefly in his brother's direction, then he shrugged his shoulders resignedly. 'Because I cannot see why it is less ill-mannered for Lucifer to leave you on a street corner,' he said, 'than for me to do so!'

It was a valid point, Rosalind recognised, and sought Lucifer's explanation, as the Contessa did, by looking at him curiously. Having consumed the last of his meal, Lucifer picked up his wine glass and drank down the dry white Falerno in one great draught before he deigned to answer. With his head tipped back and his strong brown throat exposed as he swallowed the wine, that earthy, sensual element about him became even more pronounced, and Rosalind felt the rapid tap-tapping of her heartbeat as she watched him.

Putting down his empty glass at last, he turned his black eyes on her, his long fingers still curled about the glass's fragile stem. 'I have no intention of leaving the *signorina* on a street corner,' he informed Luigi coolly. 'I will, of course, accompany her wherever she wishes to go, if she is agreeable.' The black eyes challenged her, a deep unfathomable glow in their depths. '*Passo, signorina?*' he asked quietly, and she nodded, trying hard to appear cool and unaffected.

'Sì, tante grazie, signore!'

'Buono!' It was obvious that her use of Italian won his approval, and for a moment she could almost have forgotten that there was anyone else in the room with them.

A warm flush coloured her cheeks and she could feel her fingers curl tightly round the stem of her wine glass, her eyes hastily lowered before that brilliant black gaze. She was made aware of the Contessa's interest when her cool, gnarled fingers touched her hand lightly and startled her. Turning swiftly, she recognised curiosity and a hint of speculation in the Contessa's dark eyes before she hastily concealed her own.

'You wish to go shopping, do you not, cara?' the Contessa enquired, and she hesitated, wondering whether Lucifer was prepared to go to the lengths of accompanying her round the dress shops.

With Luigi she would have had no hesitation, for he would have cheerfully come shopping and then taken her to do a little sightseeing afterwards, with Lucifer, she was less sure that he would be willing to fall in with her plans. 'I was thinking of buying a dress,' she said, glancing at him to see what his reaction would be.

He was not deterred, as she half expected him to be, but seemed to take it in his stride. 'If you wish to buy a dress then do so, signorina,' he told her. 'I am at your service.'

'Try Claudia Gerolamo, cara,' Luigi suggested very softly, and the silence that followed his words was pregnant with meaning, although no one looked at anyone else for several seconds.

Rosalind remembered seeing the name. On her only other visit to Naples during daylight hours, she recalled seeing a small but exclusive-looking shop on the Via Chiaia with the name Claudia Gerolamo scrawled across the façade in gold. It was a well-known name and everything there would no doubt be far more expensive than she had planned for, but she was tempted by the idea.

Lucifer poured himself more wine and took a drink before he made any reply, but there was a slight suggestion of hardness in his voice when he spoke, Rosalind thought. 'Of course we can try Claudia Gerolamo's if the *signorina* wishes,' he said, and flicked a dark brow in her direction. 'That suits your wishes, Signorina Matthews?'

'Oh, yes, of course!' The sudden tenseness in the atmosphere still puzzled her and she wondered what there was about Claudia Gerolamo that should not have been raised.

Looking at Luigi, she thought she detected a glint of malice in his eyes. 'You have not seen Claudia for some time,' he observed. 'She will be surprised when you walk in with Rosalinda, huh?'

'You think so?' Lucifer asked coolly, and Luigi glanced hastily at his grandmother, as if seeking her support.

If the allusion had been made with the idea of embarrassing his brother, Luigi must be feeling sadly disappointed, but no one should have known better that Lucifer Mendori was not easily discomfited. If there was something to do with

Claudia Gerolamo that was best left unmentioned, then it had had little outward effect on him, although Rosalind was undeniably curious.

The Contessa's slowly shaking head advised Luigi not to press the matter further and he shrugged, his good-looking face betraying a sulky resentment of his brother's calm. One arm resting on the table, Lucifer sipped his wine and looked at him with a glint of challenge in his black eyes, but saying nothing.

'You will not go to Gerolamo, Luca *caro*?' the Contessa's gentle voice suggested, and Lucifer smiled.

It was the smile that always reminded Rosalind of that bronze satyr beside the front doors and she felt a strange curling sensation in her stomach as she saw it. 'Of course, Nonna,' he said quietly. 'The *signorina* wishes to go, and she will not be disappointed, I am sure. Why should I not take her?'

The Contessa's shrug echoed Luigi's resignation and she smiled at Rosalind and shook her head. 'Gerolamo is an excellent designer, *bambina*,' she assured her, and Rosalind acknowledged the fact without betraying that the famous designer was also probably well out of her price range.

'I know of her, of course, Contessa,' she said. 'I think everyone does—every woman, at least.'

'You will find something to suit you.'

'Yes, yes, I'm sure I shall!'

Rosalind picked up her wine glass and emptied it. She had to go to Claudia Gerolamo, whatever happened, for she just had to see the woman who could cause such an emotion-charged silence among the Mendori family. If only she was not too expensive, she thought ruefully, and wondered what excuse she would make if she could find nothing in her price range.

CHAPTER SIX

THE soft pale pink suited her, Rosalind knew, just as the cut of the dress flattered her figure and legs when it swirled out softly as she walked. It was a dress that she had looked upon until now as her best one, mostly because it had cost more than any of her others, but also because it suited her so well. She had put it on because she felt that being escorted by Lucifer Mendori called for nothing less than the best she had.

Her long fair hair had become almost white-blonde after more than seven weeks in the Italian sun, and her fair skin had tanned to a flattering light gold. The Italian climate suited her and she had never looked or felt better in her life than she did at the moment. Giving her reflection a last complacent look, she smiled to herself and realised that the excitement she felt shone vividly in her blue eyes and made them glow.

The prospect of shopping with Lucifer excited her quite absurdly, and she tried hard to still the curling thrill it caused in her stomach as she turned to go. Hurrying along the gallery, she wondered if she was much too early or had taken too long to get ready, then, just before she reached the arched access to the stairs, she pulled herself up sharply and gave herself a mental shake. Walking with casual deliberation, she continued on her way and went through the arch as if she had all the time in the world.

Lucifer was just coming from the *salon*, having already seen Luigi on his way to keep his appointment with Signor Caccino, and he looked at her with that steady, black-eyed scrutiny she remembered from their first meeting. There was neither approval nor disapproval in his expression, but a glint in his eyes compensated for his lack of verbal response.

He wore a formal suit of pale grey with a white shirt but no tie, and the touch of informality somehow pleased her because it suggested that he was not simply sparing her time from his working day but devoting himself entirely to her, and she liked the idea of that.

The Contessa viewed their departure with mixed feelings, Rosalind thought, and she wondered if she altogether approved of Lucifer taking such an unprecedented step as to escort one of their employees. There had been little time to say much to Luigi before she went upstairs to change, but during the few minutes she had had with him he had complained about his brother's behaviour. Lucifer had no right to steal his girl, was how Luigi put it; he had never done so before and he could not imagine what he hoped to gain by doing so now.

Rosalind could not imagine either what had possessed him to suggest he take her shopping when it would have been just as easy to run Luigi into Naples and make sure he kept his appointment with Signor Caccino, but she had no desire to delve too deeply into his motives. She told herself she was a fool to be so excited about the outing, but the feeling was unquenchable and there was nothing she could do about it.

She had made the drive to Naples only once before in daylight, with Luigi, and she enjoyed it, speeding along the motorway past the multiplicity of growing crops that stretched in every direction. There were miles of fruit and vegetables ripening in the warm sun. Besides the citrus fruits she was now so used to, with their heady perfumes, there were apples and pears and peaches, almonds and olives, all growing against a background of misty hills and the ever-present, glowering mass of Vesuvius.

It was all so lush and fruitful, so warm and earthy, and it affected her strangely as she glanced at the man beside her. That strong, sensual satyr's face seemed to belong in this fruitful land, although it would have been hardly less effective elsewhere. In profile the chiselled features and arrogant Roman nose presented her with a picture she had seen many times before on old coins. That sublime head would once have worn the wreath of a conqueror, she thought, and hastily snatched herself back from letting the fantasy go too far. Lucifer Mendori was proving an intoxicating companion.

Sitting close beside him in the car, there was little she could do about the occasional contact with him, but her heart responded every time to the sensation. To the sudden pressure of his thigh when she inadvertently swayed against him and the vigorous, masculine warmth that tingled through her at every light touch.

He was a good driver too, as she would have expected, his strong hands firmly and confidently in control of the big car, displaying only a touch of the flamboyance that characterised Luigi's driving. Lucifer was a man who would scorn too much flamboyance and put his confidence rather in his own competent strength. It suddenly occurred to her as they sped along the motorway that with so much to see around her, she was giving as much attention to her companion as to her surroundings, and once more she hastily pulled herself up short.

All too soon they were running into the outskirts of Naples itself, and the less attractive aspects of the city. Even Naples had its slums and these were different from those anywhere else in the world only in that the residents were much more garrulously cheerful, and less affected by their environment. Neapolitans could be cheerful even in the most cheerless surroundings, she had discovered.

They had spoken little during the drive, and in one way it was a relief, for she would have found it difficult to know just what to talk to him about. He pointed out various industrial developments on the outskirts of Naples and seemed quite amused when she expressed surprise at seeing them. It was not all orange groves and gardens, he reminded her, and somehow managed to convey a suggestion of mockery for her innocence in such matters.

They parked the car and were walking along the Via Chiaia when he turned and looked down at her, bringing an instinctive smile to her face. Briefly he revealed white teeth in a smile that did strangely disturbing things to her self-control, his black eyes searching her face for a moment before he spoke.

'The Contessa tells me that I am thoughtless to bring you here, to Claudia Gerolamo's,' he informed her, as if he did not believe it. 'If you would rather not go there, please do not hesitate to say so, hmm?'

'Oh, but of course I want to!' Rosalind assured him. How could she resist seeing the famous Gerolamo now that she was here? Especially when she suspected there had been something between her and Lucifer—perhaps that there still was.

He nodded, then slid a hand beneath her arm suddenly and guided her across the pavement towards the doors of the *salon* she remembered. Had she been alone she would probably have hesitated at that point, but as it was she had no choice but to walk straight in. Lucifer Mendori always made an entrance.

From the outside appearance she would have expected a small, rather cramped place, but in fact the *salon* was large and luxurious beyond its double doors and she could feel her heart thudding anxiously at her ribs. Almost before they had crossed the threshold a woman stepped forward swiftly to meet them.

Tall and fashionably thin, she was striking rather than pretty or beautiful. High cheekbones and bright dark eyes and a mouth that was full and sensuous, even before she smiled, would have made her impossible to overlook even in a crowded room, but the most distinctive feature about her was her hair. It was red—not a subtle shade of auburn but frankly red, a colour that obviously disguised a natural brunette, for her complexion was the smooth dark olive-brown of the typical Neapolitan.

Her recognition of Lucifer was instant, and she made no secret of her pleasure when she saw him, although she was discreet enough to draw him swiftly into the concealment of heavy velvet drapes out of sight of her assistant and a middle-aged client, before she greeted him. She raised her arms and the full sleeves of her dress fell back as she encircled his neck, standing on tiptoe to kiss him lightly with that voluptuous mouth.

'Lucifer, *carissima!*' Her husky voice reached Rosalind clearly, and she felt suddenly deserted, finding herself alone in the middle of that luxurious *salon*.

The décor was as exotic as its owner, lushly baroque as the décor at the Villa Mimosa was and rather overpowering. Huge gilded mirrors covered most of the wall space, wherever there was room between the velvet-draped fitting rooms and display models, and even the ceiling was decorated with gilded cupids and curlicues. Mock candles shed a soft yellow light over the whole place and a deep-piled red carpet deadened every suggestion of sound other than that of the human voice.

The voice of the red-haired woman crooned softly, contentedly in Italian, and Rosalind saw Lucifer's dark head bend suddenly as he kissed her—a kiss that was followed by a long, deep exaggerated sigh of satisfaction. Then the voice went on, murmuring in Italian, while Lucifer answered in the same tongue and Rosalind could distinguish only the occasional word. The little she understood suggested that they had once been lovers and that the red-haired woman still hoped they were, and Rosalind found it embarrassing being an unwitting eavesdropper.

The assistant attending to the one other client was attempting to do her job and at the same time listen to what was being said, although it was doubtful if she could hear anything at all from where she was. Her occasional glance in Rosalind's direction was both puzzled and speculative, and Rosalind felt herself growing angry. It was no more than a minute since they came into the shop, but in the circumstances it seemed much longer.

At last she saw Lucifer turn and pull the enfolding arms from his neck, shaking his head as he moved away. The red-haired woman followed him, her mouth pouting sulkily, and she looked at Rosalind with arched brows, her dark eyes curious and unfriendly.

'Claudia,' Lucifer said coolly, 'I want you to meet Signorina Rosalind Matthews from England. *Signorina,* this is Signora Claudia Gerolamo.'

So she was married, this voluptuous, red-haired friend of his! That certainly gave a new slant to the situation and Rosalind wondered how the Contessa viewed the affair, for it was obvious that there either had been, or still was, an affair. It was probably over, at least as far as Lucifer was concerned, judging by his manner towards her—a kind of friendly affection rather than any hint of passion.

'Signorina Matthews wishes to buy a dress, Claudia,' he said, as if he had taken charge of the matter. 'You will find her something suitable I am sure, huh?'

'*Signorina!*' Claudia Gerolamo's dark eyes swept over her with a professional keenness and she nodded. 'What is it that you have in mind, *signorina?*' she asked, and her English was very strongly accented.

Rosalind shrugged. 'Just a short dress, *signora,*' she said, uneasily aware that Lucifer was still taking an interest and looked as if he might even take a personal hand in choosing her purchase. 'A—a kind of day dress, but something a little more dressy than the one I have on.'

Claudia Gerolamo swept her critical eye over the pale pink dress and her lip curled visibly. '*Naturalmente!* This was not created by me!' she said, and her accent seemed stronger than ever as she pronounced judgement. 'I would never create such a garment, *signorina,* but I will bring one that will be you—*perfezione!*'

'Thank you.' It was difficult not to object to the scornful disparagement of her favourite dress, but Rosalind forbore to say anything, partly because she lacked the requisite nerve and partly because she did not know how Lucifer would react to her telling off his friend.

She watched as the red-haired woman disappeared into the nether regions of the *salon* somewhere, and glanced at Lucifer. He seemed content to wait for as long as it took to choose a dress, but he indicated one of three velvet-upholstered chairs behind him, evidently put there for the use of accompanying males while the women were trying on dresses, and Rosalind suddenly experienced a curious sense of intimacy in their situation.

'*Permesso!*' he said, and sat down without waiting for her brief nod. Leaning back, he drew up one foot until the ankle rested on his knee. He looked relaxed and perfectly at ease so that Rosalind was driven to wondering how much time he had spent in dress *salons* waiting for a woman to buy a dress.

Claudia Gerolamo returned almost at once, carrying a pale blue dress with sprigs of lilac flowers scattered over it. It was demure and almost childish, and yet it looked ultra-feminine and Rosalind found it exquisite. One touch of her fingers was enough to tell her that it was made of pure silk and she shook her head almost without realising she was doing it because she knew without doubt that it was going to be much too expensive.

'You do not like it?' Claudia Gerolamo asked, and sounded as if she did not believe it. She had a reputation for knowing just the right dress for any client, and Rosalind realised what she had done.

'Oh, I love it, of course,' she said. 'It's beautiful!' Her fingers once more slid through the softness of the material. 'It's pure silk, isn't it?'

'Naturalmente!' The dark eyes glanced at Lucifer and Claudia Gerolamo frowned. She said something to him in Italian and he smiled and shrugged, not visibly affected by her obvious annoyance.

Then he looked up at Rosalind and arched a brow. 'Try it on, Rosalinda, huh?' he urged, and Rosalind felt the flood of colour that warmed her cheeks suddenly at the familiar nickname.

He had never before been anything but strictly formal, and she found his sudden change disconcerting. Anxious to hide her unexpected blushes from the eagle eye of both the assistant and her client, she turned quickly and went into one of the fitting rooms with Claudia Gerolamo following closely on her heels.

How could she behave like a silly schoolgirl in front of strangers simply because he had used the Italian version of her christian name? She was angry with herself and, in some perverse way, angry with him for springing it on her and taking her by surprise, although he could hardly have known what her reaction would be.

The dress fitted her perfectly, of course, Claudia Gerolamo knew her job well, but it was bound to be much too expensive and she wondered how she was going to convey as much to the other woman. That her refusal had nothing whatever to do with disliking her creation—it was simply a matter of economics.

Looking at her reflection, she felt her heart skipping wildly, the colour still high in her cheeks as she smoothed her hands down the soft fullness of the skirt. It was such a temptation to say she would have it, and yet she hadn't enough money with her to buy a dress like this. It would be not only foolish but criminal to take something she knew she could not afford.

'*Signorina?*' To her surprise the dark eyes now smiled at her via the long gilt mirror and she found herself smiling in return. She could not deny that she liked the dress and felt good in it, and the fact showed in her eyes.

'It's beautiful,' she said, stroking the softness of the silk. 'I'd love to have it—I don't see how I'm going to resist it!'

'Ah, *bene*!' Claudia Gerolamo clasped her long expressive hands together, her eyes shining in triumph. 'I knew the *signorina* would not resist! Such a garment was made for you, hmm? Whenever you wear it everyone will——' She bunched her long fingers together and kissed their tips, extending her arm to its full length in a gesture of abandon. 'Never do I fail to find just the dress for everyone! Any woman, anywhere in the world, will know you have been dressed by Gerolamo when you wear this!'

Rosalind stared at her for a moment, her whole

body growing suddenly cold when she realised what had happened. A combination of her own enthusiasm and Claudia Gerolamo's ignorance of everyday English had brought them to a hopeless misunderstanding. Her heart thudded anxiously at her side when she thought of Lucifer sitting out there waiting for her. He had told her not to be afraid of saying if something was too expensive for her, but she had somehow become entangled in a situation she could not get out of without a great deal of embarrassment all round.

It was the thought of Lucifer that finally decided her on a way out of her difficulty. He was her employer, to all intents and purposes, and there was no real reason why she should not ask him to let her have a loan against her next month's salary, even though she was not yet due to draw her second pay cheque. She would do it as discreetly as possible and try to do it without Claudia Gerolamo knowing, although that might prove difficult.

Rosalind spun round in front of the mirror once more while the creator of the dress smiled approvingly, her dark eyes glinting with satisfaction. 'I think I'll show Signor Mendori,' Rosalind said, attempting to sound casual about it, 'and see what he thinks.'

Claudia Gerolamo caught her eye again via the mirror, her own dark eyes slightly narrowed. 'It is important that he likes it?' she asked, and Rosalind felt that betraying colour in her cheeks again.

'Oh, no, not really important,' she denied a little

breathlessly, 'but I'd like someone else's opinion too!'

'The man's view, not so?' Claudia Gerolamo asked, and there was a hint of steel in the deep, expressive voice.

'Something like that,' Rosalind agreed uneasily. Asking for that loan was going to be much more difficult than she had anticipated if the other woman took such a close interest in her every move.

Once more the dark gaze held hers via the mirror and there was a bright glitter of curiosity there that made it plain she had no idea just who Rosalind was. 'You stay at the Villa Mimosa, *signorina*?' she asked, and Rosalind wondered what had stopped Lucifer making it quite plain that she worked for him.

She made no explanation, but simply answered the question, getting a certain perverse satisfaction from the other woman's curiosity. 'Yes,' she said. 'I've been there for about six weeks now.'

The dark eyes glittered and Claudia Gerolamo's red head tipped back, thrusting out her chin as she led the way from the fitting room. 'So!' she said, as if everything was crystal clear to her suddenly.

Lucifer looked up when they came into the *salon* and his black eyes immediately swept over Rosalind in one of those frank and disconcerting appraisals that brought swift colour to her cheeks once more and set her pulses racing hard. His head nodded slowly and he smiled.

'*Bella!*' he said softly. '*Vero bella!*' He looked at

Claudia Gerolamo and nodded approval, then spoke to her in their own tongue, too rapidly for Rosalind to follow, but the red-headed woman shrugged a little sulkily, looking at him from the corners of her eyes as she answered him.

Rosalind, anxious to have his attention without Claudia Gerolamo overhearing, licked her lips nervously as she waited for an opportunity. She stood with her hands in front of her, looking unconsciously prim in the soft, rather demure dress, her fair hair falling about her face as she bent her head and studied her feet.

It was Lucifer's enquiring voice that brought her head up and she took a deep breath as she prepared to explain her need for a loan against her next month's salary to pay for the dress. 'The dress is to your liking, Rosalinda?' he asked, and it was evident that he suspected something was on her mind the way he was looking at her. 'Is anything wrong?' he asked, and got to his feet as she shook her head.

'Not exactly,' Rosalind said, her voice faltering. 'I mean, if——' She broke off, looking at Claudia Gerolamo anxiously.

The red-haired woman was looking at her suspiciously and Lucifer had the expression that usually foretold impatience, so that she hastily sought words to explain. '*Signorina*,' he said quietly, 'will you tell me what is wrong, *per piacere*!'

'If—if I could speak to you,' Rosalind ventured, praying that the other woman would go without her having to ask her to.

Lucifer glanced at Claudia Gerolamo, then raised a brow as he looked down at Rosalind. 'You wish to speak to me alone?' he asked, and Rosalind nodded. He murmured a few words in Italian and Claudia Gerolamo glanced quickly from one to the other, then thrust out her chin and tossed her red head as she walked across the *salon* out of earshot. 'Now,' Lucifer said, 'we are alone, you may say what you have to say!'

Rosalind wished he would at least unbend sufficiently to use her christian name again, but he simply looked down at her with his black eyes deep and unfathomable and she felt small and incredibly foolish as she stood there in front of him. The softness of the silk under her hands reminded her of what she had to say, and she clasped her fingers tightly and nervously together.

'Signor Mendori,' she began, and again licked her lips anxiously before she went on. 'I—I find I haven't enough money with me to pay for this dress.'

She looked up at him anxiously and he regarded her with his black brows raised. 'And you must, of course, have that particular one,' he said, making it a statement of fact instead of a question, as he so often did.

Rosalind looked down at the dress, its soft folds clinging to her figure, emphasising it, flattering it and making her feel as if she would never look as good in anything again. 'It—it seems so right for me, somehow,' she said, half apologetically, and he still regarded her steadily.

'*Perfetto*,' he agreed quietly.

Rosalind drew a deep breath. 'I wondered if you would—if I could perhaps—borrow against my next month's salary,' she said.

Lucifer said nothing for a second, and she felt her heart turn cold in anticipation of his refusal, her hands curling with embarrassment as he looked down at her. Then suddenly a strong hand was thrust beneath her chin and she was forced to look at him, while his thumb moved slowly and sensuously on her soft skin, his black eyes studying her.

'That is all that troubles you?' he asked, and she would have nodded her head had it been possible.

'I wondered if you'd mind,' she said in a husky whisper, feeling more confident now. She was aware that Claudia Gerolamo was watching them closely, even though she could not hear what was being said and heaven knew what she was making of his present attitude.

'Of course you shall have the money,' he told her quietly. His black eyes watched her for a moment and there was a suggestion of a smile in their depths, then he looked down at her mouth and kept his gaze there with an intensity that stirred her heart into violent action. 'I would offer to make it a gift,' he said, 'but you would not allow that, would you, Rosalinda?'

Rosalind's heart gave a great lurch of disbelief and she raised her eyes swiftly, wide and startled, trying to determine what had possessed him to make such an offer. Surely it was not done simply with the idea of impressing her with his generosity, such a supposition would not do him justice. But the warmth in his eyes suggested another reason and she dared not dwell on that possibility.

She could well imagine how the Contessa would react if she learned that Lucifer was buying expensive dresses for her and, apart from the fact that the Contessa would know a dress like that was beyond her means, she would have to admit who had paid for it. She would never be able to keep up the deception if she did not, and with the plans for choosing Lucifer a bride well under way the gift would be viewed with twice the suspicion.

Almost reluctantly she shook her head, her chin confined by the strength of his fingers. 'No, thank you, Signor Mendori,' she said huskily. 'I couldn't let you do that.'

She thought she saw speculation in his eyes suddenly, and the fingers holding her chin tightened imperceptibly. 'Would you also have refused Luigi?' he asked in a voice quiet enough not to be audible to anyone but her, and she reached up and pushed away his hand, her eyes bright and reproachful.

He always seemed so ready to blame Luigi whenever she expressed doubt about letting him do anything for her, as when he wanted her to learn Italian, and it made her curious that he was so ready to believe his brother meant so much more to her. It was almost as if he was jealous of Luigi—but that suspicion she hastily dismissed as unlikely.

'It has nothing to do with Luigi at all,' she told

him, keeping her own voice inaudible to anyone else. 'It wouldn't matter who you were, I'm still independent enough to buy my own dresses!'

'Ah!'

Strangely enough he sounded more satisfied with her tirade than angry and she glanced at him from the corners of her eyes, her heart fluttering rapidly. 'You should know that about me by now,' she ventured, and he smiled.

'I thought I did,' he said, and Rosalind stood looking at him, a dark glint of satisfaction gleaming in his eyes. Had there ever, she wondered, been a more complex man than Lucifer Mendori? She had certainly never met anyone like him in her life before.

He shook his head and reached inside his jacket for his cheque book. 'I shall make a cheque for the price of the dress,' he informed her. 'You may look upon it as an advance against your next month's salary.' He smiled briefly. 'That at least will ensure that you do not desert the Contessa!'

Having been given the impression that she was buying the dress herself, then seeing him produce his cheque book, Claudia Gerolamo arched her fine brows and advanced with the taut, careful grace of a cat, her dark eyes curious and suspicious.

'*Quanto costa*, Claudia?' he asked, but she did not immediately answer.

Eyes narrowed and glittering, she looked at Rosalind as if she would have torn the dress from her and flung the pieces at Lucifer in her anger. She asked a question in Italian that Rosalind was not quick enough to translate, and Lucifer's black eyes narrowed sharply.

'*Quanto costa l'abito*, Claudia?' he insisted, and Claudia Gerolamo glared at him angrily, until presumably her business instincts overcame her resentment and she murmured a price that was quite fantastically expensive, even for a model, and made Rosalind's stomach curl in alarm.

She knew the price asked was much too high and, from the way he hesitated, so did Lucifer. It was a mere suggestion of immobility, however, and then he took a pen from his pocket and began to write out the amount she had asked, his big, bold signature taking almost the whole of the bottom line of the cheque.

'Lucifer——'

A long slim hand was laid on his, as if Claudia Gerolamo already regretted her impulsive malice, but Lucifer brushed her hand aside and gave her the cheque. Then he turned to Rosalind and half smiled, once more subjecting her to that long, explicit scrutiny that could so disturb her senses.

'You will keep on the dress?' he asked, and Rosalind looked down at it, her hands smoothing the soft silk, wondering if she dared wear it very much now that she had it, for fear of spoiling it in some way.

'Shall I?' she asked impulsively. 'I'd like to, I feel good in it.'

'So!' He shrugged his broad shoulders and half smiled. 'Such confidence is worth much to a woman, hmm?'

Rosalind thought uneasily about the cheque still in Claudia Gerolamo's hand and speculated on how long it would take her to pay back the money. 'Almost,' she agreed with a rather doubtful smile. She glanced at Claudia Gerolamo, just behind him. 'If Signora Gerolamo will be kind enough to pack up my other dress,' she said, and instinctively angled her chin as she met the red-haired woman's resentful eyes. 'I'm very fond of that dress, even though it isn't high fashion!'

Without a word Claudia Gerolamo turned and walked back into the fitting room, returning only seconds later with the pink dress in one of her own dress bags. It was probably something she would rather not have had to do, Rosalind thought, in view of her opinion of the dress. Rosalind took it with a nod of thanks, then turned to see if Lucifer was ready to leave now that their mission was accomplished.

Claudia Gerolamo had a hand on his arm and she was looking at him with unmistakable appeal in her dark eyes. It was possible for Rosalind to realise how she felt to some extent, for she obviously felt very intensely about him and, unless she had misjudged Lucifer Mendori, he had very little left for her. She could imagine that he was an exciting and passionate lover, but he would show little compassion once it was all over.

'Lucifer, *posso riverderla*?' she asked, and Rosalind found her plea oddly touching.

Lucifer smiled, a small, understanding smile, and there was a surprisingly gentle look on his satyr-like features as he looked down at her. Then he placed his hand over hers and gently disengaged it, uncurling the slim fingers and holding them in his for a moment. Bending his head, he pressed his lips to her forehead.

'*Addio*, Claudia,' he said quietly. '*Sono sicuro che ci incontreremo di nuovo!*'

I'm sure we'll run into each other again some time! It was said gently, but the finality of it was unmistakable and Rosalind felt herself curl inwardly, not daring to look at Claudia Gerolamo. Instead she turned and walked towards the street doors, anxious not to see the effect of that kindly but inexorable dismissal. Lucifer was beside her in a moment, opening the doors for her, not even turning his head to look back.

Rosalind stepped through into the street, blinking for a second in the sudden brightness of the sunshine, but before Lucifer could follow her out something came hurtling in his wake and crashed harshly against the metal edge of the door. Startled, she turned quickly. Lucifer was half turned too, one hand on the door, a tiny trickle of blood running down the back of his fingers, looking down at the shattered vase on the red carpet.

It was like a tableau set out in the exotic dimness of the *salon*. The startled and curious assistant and her client both staring towards the doors, and behind them, like a vivid, angry figure of vengeance, Claudia Gerolamo, her red head tipped back and her dark eyes glittering with fury. No one moved but seemed to be in a state of suspended animation, looking after Rosalind and Lucifer.

Then Lucifer urged her forward and let the doors swing to behind them, the warmth of his large palm tingling to her skin through the soft silk dress. 'Would you like to do a little sightseeing now?' he asked coolly.

CHAPTER SEVEN

IT was quite late when they returned to the Villa Mimosa, in fact it was almost dinner time and much later than Rosalind had expected to be. Luigi, she knew, was bound to say something, for he had not approved of the outing with Lucifer in the first place, and the fact that she had enjoyed herself so much that she was late back would be adding insult to injury. Not that she felt she had to explain herself to anyone, she decided. Lucifer had volunteered to take her and he had chosen the places they visited.

Naples had proved fascinating with Lucifer as a guide, for he took her to places that Luigi would have found dull. During the one daytime trip she had made to Naples before, Luigi had willingly taken her round the shops and to a restaurant, but he had shrugged off suggestions that they visit the historical places.

With Lucifer it had been quite different. They

had visited churches and museums and the impressive Castel Nuovo on the waterfront that he had told her was built during the time of Charles the First of Anjou in the thirteenth century. Finally they had driven up to Certosa di San Martino, an old Carthusian monastery which housed a National Museum with some of Naples' most beautiful treasures. More than that, it offered from its balcony what Lucifer claimed was the best possible view of Naples itself, down the slopes of the Vomero to the bay.

She felt tired but strangely contented as they drove back and she got out of the car with Lucifer's hand under her arm, his strong fingers curved into her soft flesh. The blue silk dress floated about her slim legs as she stood up and she was once more reminded of the incident its purchase had caused. Nothing remained of the cut on Lucifer's hand but a faint hairline of dried blood, but nevertheless she hastily avoided looking at it, and tried to decide yet again whether or not he had deserved that furious parting shot.

There was no time to bath and change before dinner—not that Rosalind had intended changing out of her new dress. A hasty wash and a brush through her long hair was all that was needed to make her perfectly presentable, and she took a last look at her reflection in the mirror, then hurried from the room, glancing at her wristwatch as she turned to close the door. She was brought up sharply when she collided with someone coming from further along the gallery, and her heart began to pound violently when she realised who it must be.

Somehow Lucifer had found time to shave as well, and put on a tie, and the warmth of his body mingled with the fresh smell of aftershave as she was held by her upper arms and turned round. She looked up, ready to apologise, but instead of the expression she expected to see, there was a different, disturbing look that glittered in his black eyes and set her pulse racing more wildly than ever.

His strong fingers held her firm and for a second he looked down at her with that curiously luminous look, then suddenly and without warning she was pulled against him. His arms were around her, steel-hard and irresistible, one hand twined into her hair, pulling back her head until her mouth was turned up to him, her lips parted in surprise.

His mouth was hard and had a kind of hungry passion that drew every atom of resistance from her. Not that she offered resistance, only curled her hands against the broad warmth of his back and yielded to what her heart told her was what she wanted more than anything in the world.

He moulded her soft shape to his own hard leanness, and the strong curve of his fingers cradling her head allowed no fraction of movement. For several seconds she even forgot where she was, and the frankly sensuous longing she felt for the man who aroused such passion in her was the only thing she was aware of.

The voice, when she eventually became aware of it, came from somewhere behind her and she murmured a wordless and half-hearted protest against the mouth that still possessed her own. She registered her name and then a stunned silence in the moment that Lucifer released her, and she turned swiftly, his hands letting her go reluctantly, it seemed.

Luigi stood at the top of the stairs, just beyond the archway, and the shadowed light of the gallery lent a certain ageing gauntness to his good looks. 'Luigi!' She looked at him, her eyes still dazed and a shining deep violet blue between half-lowered lashes.

For a moment he stood looking at them along the gallery from the archway and his expression was almost as dazed as her own. Then he came towards them, his dark eyes switching curiously from one to the other. It came as a shock when he laughed suddenly, and Rosalind stared at him unbelievingly, a flush on her cheeks.

'*Dio mio!*' he said with unmistakable malice. 'What will Nonna think of this, I wonder, huh?'

Lucifer interrupted sharply, speaking in Italian which was much too quick for Rosalind to follow apart from recognising one or two words which gave her the general gist of his meaning. It was no wonder Luigi flushed and curled his hands into fists as he stood there and glared defiance at him. Once more she felt pity for him, for he never seemed to learn not to cross swords with his brother.

It was pure instinct that made her reach out and touch his arm, her first thought for the Contessa's well-laid plans and what her reaction might be.

'Please, Luigi,' she said, her eyes anxious, 'there's no need to tell the Contessa!'

She knew that Lucifer was watching her, made curious by her obvious anxiety that the Contessa should not know he had kissed her. Luigi, of course, was fully aware of her reasons and he smiled, his teeth gleaming in the brown smoothness of his face as he stood looking at her. 'You think *la mia nonna* will not like to hear of you kissing with Lucifer?' he asked. 'Well, I too do not like it, *carissima*! Why did you not wait and let me drive you to Napoli, huh? Did you think it would be more—interesting with Lucifer?'

'Oh, Luigi, please don't!' Rosalind was growing angry now as well as anxious and she looked at him with bright, dark eyes.

He swept his gaze over the new blue dress. 'Ah, you have met *la* Gerolamo! She is—mmm! Huh?' He rolled his eyes and used his hands with unmistakable meaning, then lightly touched her shoulder with one finger. Stroking the soft pale silk, he smiled. 'You have been *stravagante, cara mia*,' he said, and looked directly at his brother, his eyes still glittering malice. 'Or perhaps you were not troubled by prices, eh?' It was the look in Lucifer's eyes that eventually quelled him and he stood there for a moment longer, then nodded his head and looked at Rosalind with a hint of apology. 'If I am mistaken, Rosalinda,' he told her, his English much more strongly accented than usual, 'I apologise!'

She smiled, glad it was over, but still wondering

rather uneasily if he would be ready to let the matter drop completely or if he would find the temptation to inform the Contessa too much to resist. 'It doesn't matter, Luigi,' she said. 'Just forget about it.'

He glanced at his brother again before he answered her, bobbing his head in a slight bow. '*Naturalmente*,' he said, and glanced at his wristwatch. 'I am to inform you that dinner is ready to be served when you come.'

'Oh yes, of course, we're late!' Rosalind too looked at the time, then made to follow him. 'I'm coming, Luigi!'

Lucifer's hand on her arm detained her and she turned and looked at him curiously. '*Un momento*, Rosalinda, *per favore*,' he said quietly. Luigi did not turn to see why she was not following him and they watched him disappear through the archway and go downstairs. Turning back to Lucifer, she met a deep and disturbing gaze fixed on her and detected a small frown between his black brows. 'The Contessa has seen Luigi kiss you sometimes,' he said in a cool, matter-of-fact voice. 'Is there some reason why she would not allow me the same privilege, Rosalinda?'

Hearing him use her name in the familiar surroundings of the villa somehow sounded more intimate than it had that first time, in Claudia Gerolamo's *salon*, and stirred her more deeply. Instinctively she glanced at his right hand, held loosely relaxed at his side, reminded again of the red-haired woman's fury because he had so definitely rejected her. Despite the breathtaking passion of that kiss he had surprised her with just now, she realised that she could hardly hope to fare better when he no longer found her youth and freshness as enjoyable as he evidently did at the moment.

She laughed shakily, giving no thought to how rash she was being, only rueful of her own weakness where he was concerned. Several times she had felt the urge to warn him about the Contessa's plans for his future, and now she did so without stopping to think how it could affect her own position.

'But of course the Contessa would object,' she told him, 'when she's gone to so much trouble to arrange things with the idea of finding you a——' She stopped there, realising at last what she had done, and Lucifer was looking at her closely, his black eyes glittering like coals.

'Explain, *per piacere*,' he said, and that familiar edge of steel was on his voice so that she licked her lips anxiously.

'It—it really isn't my place to explain—to say anything about it,' she said, knowing it was already too late. 'I shouldn't have said anything and I hope you won't let the Contessa know I have!'

His expression was implacable, a dark glitter in his eyes. 'You have told me nothing, *mia cara*,' he said, 'but I think that you will!'

'We have to go,' she said, anxious to escape. 'Luigi said they're waiting dinner for us!'

She would have walked off, but his strong fingers

curled relentlessly around her left wrist and held it tightly. 'Not yet, Rosalinda,' he insisted. 'There is something about which I seem to know nothing, although you and Luigi do. I mean to know what is going on in my own household, and you will tell me, *piccola!*'

'Lucifer!'

He ignored both her plea and the fact that she dispensed with the formality of Signor Mendori. 'I have not troubled myself with these plans to fill the house with visitors,' he said. 'My grandmother is entitled to have her friends to stay as often as she chooses, but now——' His eyes narrowed and the hold on her wrist relaxed until his thumb moved slowly over the smooth skin of her forearm while he gazed down at her, thoughtfully suspicious. '*Who* is coming to stay, Rosalinda?' he asked. 'Who is it, huh?'

'Several people,' she told him evasively. 'Friends of the Contessa, as you said.'

'Names, *piccola!*' he warned softly, and Rosalind knew she would tell him sooner or later.

She looked down at her captive wrist, her flesh tingling with that light, seductive caress, and then once more she licked her lips anxiously. 'There's a family from Rome coming in about three weeks' time,' she told him. 'Signor, Signora and Signorina Cassini, and soon after that a Madame Cordaire and her niece are coming from France.'

She needed to go no further, she could see that. Lucifer was nodding his head, his eyes glinting and a small tight smile drawing his mouth at one corner. 'Ah!' he said. '*Mi astuzia nonna!* She thinks to find a wife for me, eh, Rosalinda?'

'I don't know!' She tried to look away, but he put his hand under her chin and tipped her face up to look at him, his gaze resting with disturbing intensity on her mouth.

'You lie, *piccola*,' he told her quietly. 'You know a great deal, I think, about what concerns me!' Swiftly his gaze searched her face, then he smiled, a mockery of a smile that made the satyr's face look not only rueful but cruel, and Rosalind shivered. 'Have they told you that I must marry or lose everything for which I have worked, Rosalinda? Do you also know that I have less than one year in which to find myself a wife?'

It was impossible to nod her head with his hand under her chin and she could not keep the sympathy she felt from showing in her eyes as she answered him. She had never liked the idea of the Contessa finding him a wife, but she liked the thought of his losing Mendori e Figli even less. 'I know,' she whispered, and he looked down at her narrow-eyed.

'And you pity me!' he accused. He withdrew his hand from her chin as if he no longer wanted to touch her, and Rosalind simply stood saying nothing, but rubbing the marks that his fingers had left on her face. 'Do you really imagine,' he said after a moment or two of silence, 'that I would allow anyone, even the Contessa, to run my life for me? To choose my wife for me?'

'No,' Rosalind confessed huskily. 'I told the Contessa I didn't think you would.'

Briefly he smiled and the black eyes searched her face slowly. 'You think you know me so well, Rosalinda?' he asked, and she felt the colour flush into her cheeks under his scrutiny. He gave her no time to answer, but shook his head. 'When I marry,' he informed her coolly, 'I shall marry someone of my choosing, and you may tell my grandmother and my brother so, Rosalinda!'

'Oh, but I can't let them know I've told you,' she insisted hastily. 'If the Contessa knows I told you about——'

'Only under duress, *piccola*,' he reminded her, and pointed out the marks of his fingers still faint on her chin. 'I am brute enough to have forced the information from you!' He laughed shortly as he took her arm to go downstairs. 'You will find that Luigi at least will believe that!' he said.

For almost two weeks Rosalind was on tenterhooks wondering if the Contessa would learn she had told Lucifer of her plans for him. She did not think Lucifer would betray her, but just the same it would have been less trying if the whole thing had been brought into the open.

The Contessa talked of little else but the coming visits and she was so certain that one among her friends' daughters would take Lucifer's fancy enough for him to contemplate marrying her. As for Luigi, he made no effort to disguise the fact that he looked forward to having a succession of eligible girls in the house, even though he was as attentive as ever towards Rosalind now that he had recovered from his anger.

He sat with her in the garden after lunch one day, sharing a seat under one of the cypress trees, surrounded by the scents and sounds of the garden that were now so much a part of her life. 'Will you be *gelosa, carissima*?' he asked suddenly, and Rosalind looked at him curiously.

For the moment the advent of the visitors was at the back of her mind and she could not think what he referred to. 'Jealous?' she asked. 'Who should I be jealous of, Luigi?'

He smiled, lifting the long hair from her neck with gentle fingers. Then he kissed her beside her ear, a light, teasing kiss that left only a flutter of sensation in its wake. 'Giovanna Cassini,' he reminded her, 'and all the other *belle ragazze* that Nonna has invited to stay!'

Rosalind smiled and shook her head. 'Oh, those!' she said. 'Knowing you, Luigi, I wouldn't dream of being jealous, no matter how many beautiful girls the Contessa invites. No one would expect you to ignore them even if they aren't invited specifically to amuse you!'

There was speculation in Luigi's dark eyes for a moment as he watched her and he rubbed his lower lip thoughtfully with a finger. 'It will be interesting to see how my brother reacts to this—parade of brides,' he observed after a while, and there was a suggestion of malice in his smile as he pondered on the prospect. 'He will suspect nothing until it is too late, *sì*?'

'Oh, for heaven's sake, Luigi, Lucifer isn't a fool!' She sounded so angry that for a moment Luigi stared at her curiously.

His dark eyes searched her face, noting the bright flush in her cheeks and the way her eyes avoided his, then he leaned across and kissed her. 'You have told him, *bella mia*, have you not?' he asked, and Rosalind sat for a moment, regarding her clasped hands in her lap.

'I didn't mean to,' she said huskily at last. 'Although I never thought it was very fair to him. It seems so——'

Luigi kissed her mouth firmly, stemming the husky uncertainty of her explanation, then he traced the soft, trembling curve of her mouth with a fingertip. 'You are foolish, *mi piccola* Rosalinda,' he told her softly. 'Lucifer will not marry you—he would never consider it!'

'Marry me?' Rosalind looked up at him swiftly, her eyes wide, stunned by the very idea of it. She had sometimes seen the possibility of his having an affair with her, always providing she allowed things to go that far, but she had never once expected marriage to enter into his plans and she shook her head slowly. 'You have it all wrong, Luigi,' she told him, and her voice sounded oddly faint and unsteady. 'I've never for one moment expected anything—anything like that. I can't think where you got that idea!'

He looked at her curiously for a second, and she knew he was remembering her readiness to go with Lucifer to Naples rather than wait until he was free to take her, and the kiss he had interrupted after they returned. There might have been other times when she had inadvertently betrayed Lucifer's undeniable attraction for her, and she hastily avoided his eyes.

'But you would be his *amante*?' he asked, and she flushed at the frankness of the question.

'Nor will I be his mistress!' she denied.

Luigi said nothing for a moment, then he shrugged his shoulders, perhaps a little uneasily, as if he was not quite sure of his ground. 'Then I am sorry, *cara*,' he said. 'I was mistaken, but I would not like to see you hurt because you hope for the impossible—you are much too—*bella*!' He bunched his fingers and kissed their tips in an extravagant gesture that brought a smile to her eyes despite his previous suggestions.

'You're incorrigible, Luigi!' she told him, shaking her head, and he smiled.

Leaning across her, he put one hand on the back of the seat, bringing his face to within inches of hers, his dark eyes glowing. 'Much better that you love me, *carissima*,' he murmured close to her mouth. 'I am not so *importante* in the scheme of things, *sì*?'

Rosalind closed her eyes while he kissed her, unable to stop herself from comparing him with Lucifer in the same situation. When Luigi kissed her she enjoyed the experience without being too emotionally affected, but Lucifer's kiss left her breathless and lightheaded, and she wondered just how firm she really could be if ever he did want her for his *amante*.

Another few days, Rosalind thought as she looked out of her bedroom window, and the first of the visitors would be arriving. Normally she was a fairly sociable creature and she would have looked forward to the company, but the reason behind the invitations took the pleasure from her anticipation.

Although Lucifer had been so insistent that he would choose his own wife, she could not help wondering if he would eventually relinquish his principles rather than lose the business he had worked so hard to build up. She hated the idea of it happening, but it had to be considered as a possibility when there was so much at stake. Somehow she would not mind nearly so much if Luigi married for expediency.

A door closing along the gallery somewhere brought her out of her uneasy daydream and she picked up her hairbrush, surprised to see a hazy, almost tearful image reflected in the mirror. She brushed vigorously, drawing the silky blonde hair back from her forehead. 'Oh, don't be such an idiot!' she commanded her reflection.

The Contessa was already having breakfast when she went out into the garden, sharing the table with Lucifer who was going through the customary pile of mail beside his plate. Rosalind replied to their brief greetings and poured herself coffee, glancing at Lucifer from the corner of her eye as she held the cup to her lips. 'Do you need me this morning, Contessa?' she asked, and the old lady shook her head.

'Not this morning, *cara*,' she said. 'You gave me your afternoon yesterday to write letters—this morning you are free to do as you will!' The dark eyes gleamed at her with affectionate curiosity. 'You plan to go out, *bambina*?' she asked.

Rosalind nodded, putting down her cup. 'Luigi's offered to take me to a little cove he knows, just along the coast, where we can go swimming,' she said. 'It sounds lovely and I haven't been in the sea for ages!'

The Contessa seemed delighted with the plan, but Lucifer had other ideas, apparently. 'That will not be possible!' he declared flatly, and Rosalind frowned at him curiously. He did not even look up from the letter he had in his hand, but continued in the same flat, matter-of-fact voice as before. 'Luigi has an appointment today with one of our designers, Rosalinda,' he informed her. 'Taking you swimming is out of the question, I am afraid!'

'Oh!' She wasn't quite sure what she ought to say, but she felt very disappointed and her voice must have betrayed the fact, for he proceeded to offer additional reasons for Luigi's unavailability. 'It is more than a week since he was near the *ufficio*,' he told her shortly. 'He cannot be spared on this occasion!'

It sounded to Rosalind very much as if he put the blame for Luigi's absence from the office firmly on to her, and she was prepared to deny it, forcefully if necessary. 'It's not my doing that Luigi hasn't been to work,' she told him quietly. 'I haven't been out with him this week at all.'

Lucifer looked up at last, his black eyes holding hers steadily for a moment. 'I blame no one but Luigi himself, Rosalinda,' he told her, 'but I cannot free him simply because you are available to go swimming with him—*mi spiace*!'

The Contessa, sensing how she felt to some extent, reached out and covered her hand, her crippled fingers offering gentle consolation. 'You will not go swimming alone, *cara*?' she asked. 'A strange place with no one to help you if you——'

'I won't go alone, Contessa,' she assured her, and glanced across at Lucifer's unrelenting profile. 'I'll wait until Luigi's free to take me—there's plenty of time.'

'Not so much time, *bambina*,' the old lady reminded her. 'We have our first visitors arriving very soon now.'

'Oh yes, of course!' Rosalind laughed, glancing at Lucifer again with a gleam of malice in her eyes. 'Luigi won't want to take me around when the visitors are here, will he?'

It had been rash perhaps to suggest that the visitors would be of any special interest to Luigi, for that could mean only one thing, and she caught the swift, brief frown of the Contessa's, as if she feared she had been too outspoken. Lucifer was watching her with one brow raised and a glitter of amusement in his black eyes. 'But surely those pretty girls are for my benefit, are they not, *piccola*?' he suggested softly, then transferred his gaze to his grandmother. 'Is that not so, Nonna?'

He was actually enjoying it, Rosalind realised incredulously, and curled her hands more tightly around her coffee cup. Here she had been sympathising with him for being faced with a dismaying choice of marrying or losing his inheritance. She had even risked the Contessa's wrath to warn him that he was being manoeuvred into an inescapable position by his indomitable grandmother, and he gave every appearance of enjoying the situation.

From the Contessa's expression it was clear that she found it an embarrassment having her stratagem discovered, and she raised her fine brows as she carefully placed her knife on the side of her empty plate. '*Non capisco*, Luca,' she said, but Lucifer knew well enough that she understood and he was shaking his head while he poured himself more coffee.

'You think I do not know that Signor and Signora Cassini have an unmarried daughter, *cara*?' he asked gently. 'Or that Madame Cordaire has an unmarried niece? Madame Nouvel has a daughter? Also Mr. and Mrs. Delaney and Mrs. Courtney? I am not a fool, Nonna, I was bound to discover your—plan?—sooner or later, eh?'

'Adolfo posted my *lettere*, he told you their names,' the Contessa accused, and Lucifer was shaking his head slowly.

'*Carissima!*' His deep soft voice soothed the old lady's ruffled dignity with a skill that could only have come with practice and he held her hands

140

gently in his while he spoke to her, his black eyes warm and persuasive. 'I know the names of your friends, do I not?' he asked. 'And I saw your invitation list upon your *leggio*. I did not need Adolfo to tell me who was invited here, nor do I set my servants to keep watch on you!' He shook his head as if such suspicion was unworthy of her. '*Non la so*, Nonna?'

For a moment the Contessa said nothing, then she smiled at Rosalind a little ruefully. '*Mi spiace*, Rosalinda,' she said, 'but I thought that you had——' She shrugged her shoulders. 'Of course I was wrong even to think you and Adolfo would do such a thing.' She turned once more to her grandson and her eyes were gentle and a little sad as they rested on that dark satyr-like face. 'You are not angry, *caro mio*?' she asked, and Lucifer smiled.

'Only that you tried to trick me instead of telling me of your plan,' he told her. 'I know how you felt and why you did it.'

'There is so little time, *carissimo* Luca,' the old lady reminded him. 'There is so much to lose if you do not marry!'

Lucifer smiled, bending his head over her hand to kiss the gnarled fingers lightly. 'And you do not trust me to choose for myself, Nonna?' he asked without looking at her. 'You do not think I will bring you a granddaughter worthy to be the Contessa Mendori?'

He spoke so quietly that Rosalind was not even sure if she had heard him correctly at first, but the Contessa was looking at him with her dark eyes narrowed and shrewd as if she too doubted her own ears. 'You have made a choice already, *caro mio?*' she asked. She clasped her hands together tightly, her eyes briefly closed as if in prayer. 'Oh, why did you not tell me?'

'Because I have scarcely realised it myself,' Lucifer told her, 'and I cannot yet bring myself to admit it—give me a while longer, Nonna.'

'Luca——'

'I will not be hurried, Nonna,' Lucifer interrupted firmly but gently. 'It is too important a matter to me.'

'*Sì, sì—naturalmente!*' The Contessa shook her head a little dazedly. 'I know the *signorina?*' she insisted, and he took a moment, then shook his head, glancing at Rosalind as he did so.

His reticence together with that hasty, slightly uneasy glance gave Rosalind her cue. It was easy to see that he was uneasy about being too frank in front of her and too polite to speak to his grandmother in Italian. Her heart was thudding hard and anxiously at her side and she felt suddenly as if she had no place there. It was too intimate a subject to be discussed at length with a stranger there to hear every word that was said, only she had not until that moment realised that she was still a stranger.

She got to her feet suddenly, clumsy in her movements and quite alarmingly shaky. 'If you'll excuse me, Contessa,' she said, her voice small and dry, 'I'll—I'll go and get ready to go out.'

Briefly the Contessa gave her her attention. '*Sì,*

naturalmente, cara,' she told her. '*A più tarde!*'

'Rosalinda!' Lucifer's voice called after her and she turned, looking at him without meeting his eyes, it was suddenly very hard to do that. 'You are going out alone?' he asked, and she nodded.

'Yes,' she said. 'I haven't much choice if Luigi's busy, have I?' She gave him no time to say anything else but turned and hurried across the garden to the house.

She found Luigi in the hall and he looked at her curiously, puzzled by the bright flush in her cheeks and curious brittleness about her manner. '*Carissima?*' He put an arm around her shoulders and drew her to him until she was close enough to kiss, his mouth warm and teasing. 'You look unhappy,' he told her, smiling and persuasive. 'Tell me about it, will you?'

Rosalind shrugged; she did not really know herself why she felt the way she did, but she did not relish the thought of spending the whole morning in her own company. 'We can't go swimming,' she told him. 'Lucifer says you have an appointment at the office.'

The word he used was less than polite and she could guess its meaning even in Italian. He hugged her close and his dark eyes gleamed a challenge as he looked down at her. 'We will go swimming,' he declared firmly. 'Now, *carissima,* before Lucifer has time to stop us! *Presto, cara!* Fetch your things and meet me in *due minuti!*'

'But, Luigi, we can't!' She hung back against the hand that urged her towards the stairs. 'You can't walk out on another appointment—Lucifer will blame me!'

Luigi raised his eyes to heaven and spread his expressive hands in appeal. '*Dio mio,*' he pleaded, 'am I a *bambino* that I must ask my brother if I may go where I wish? And why should you be afraid of what Lucifer will say to you, *carissima*? How can he blame you if I do as I wish to do without asking him?'

Rosalind thought of Lucifer sitting out there in the garden with the Contessa, waiting to tell her about the woman he had fallen in love with but reluctant to say any more until she had gone. He had made her feel like an intruder, a stranger, and she found it hard to bear. Aware that Luigi was looking at her narrowly, puzzled by the misty brightness in her eyes, she stuck out her chin and laughed up at him.

'How *can* he blame me?' she said. 'I'll go and get my things, *caro* Luigi, and be down in a couple of minutes—don't go without me!'

CHAPTER EIGHT

IT was idyllic when they eventually arrived at Luigi's secret cove, and so far undiscovered by anyone else, or so he claimed. Nestled into a curve in the coast, it was accessible only via a steep downward path from the road and therefore unlikely to be discovered by anyone not familiar with the terrain.

The cliff face here was not cultivated as in Crisdorfi, but trees grew down the entire depth from top to bottom. The path wound its way tortuously among them, dropping steeply at every step until they came upon the little beach quite unexpectedly, leaving the cool shade for the sudden salty lustre of hot sand and an ocean that glittered like blue and gold glass with barely a ripple disturbing its surface.

It was an environment designed to encourage lazy enjoyment, and yet Rosalind found it hard to be as relaxed and carefree as she felt she ought to be. Luigi lay stretched out on the sand beside her, dressed again after their swim but with his shirt open and exposing his lean tanned torso to the sun. He looked completely at ease and seemed to have no conscience at all about the appointment he had failed to keep so that he could bring her to the cove to swim.

The sleeveless green print dress she wore made Rosalind look deceptively cool, for she was in fact uncomfortably hot and her cheeks were flushed pink beneath her tan. She sat hugging her knees and gazing at the water where it rippled lazily over the sand only a few feet from where they sat, and she would have given a lot to be able to forget those last few minutes with Lucifer and the Contessa, but somehow she couldn't.

After all the times she had wished he could find and marry a woman he loved instead of being faced with either losing the business or marrying some-one he could see only as a means to an end, it was ridiculous to feel the way she did, but she simply could not help it.

She sighed, though quite involuntarily, and Luigi opened his eyes and looked up at her. 'Rosa-linda?' He sat up and put an arm around her shoulders, leaning across to kiss her, then lifting her chin and smiling down at her curiously. 'Why such a big sigh, *carissima*?' he asked. 'Are you not happy?'

Rosalind smiled, avoiding the hand under her chin. 'Yes, of course I'm happy,' she said. 'It's lovely here and I've really enjoyed my swim.'

'Ah, you think it was worth playing—how do you say?—truant, hmm?'

Rosalind turned her head, looking down at her hand as she sifted grains of warm sand through her fingers. 'I wish you hadn't, Luigi,' she said. 'There's bound to be trouble when Lucifer finds out you've broken another appointment.'

He shrugged with a bravado she could not quite believe in and grinned at her. '*Forse*, but I am not sorry I came, *carissima*, and I hope you are not.'

'I feel horribly guilty,' Rosalind confessed, 'al-though I have no need to, it's you who's playing truant, not me!'

'*Naturalmente!* So why do you make yourself unhappy, then?'

'I suppose because, unlike you, I have a con-science,' she told him, and looked at him anxiously when he stroked her bottom lip gently with one finger before he kissed her. 'Luigi, why don't you take more interest in the business, like Lucifer does?'

He studied her for a second seriously, then kissed her lips again and smiled, his forehead pressed to hers while he spoke. 'Maybe because I am lazy?' he suggested softly, and laughed. 'I leave the work to Lucifer because he likes to do it and I do not—that is a good reason, no?'

His persuasiveness was irresistible and she shook her head, smiling ruefully. 'I suppose it is,' she said.

'Oh, Rosalinda! *Mia bella* Rosalinda!' He leaned forward and kissed her neck, turning her round to face him again. 'You will smile for me, *sì*?' he coaxed softly. 'You have no need to be sad, *cara*, and I hate to see you so. I will make you happy, hmm?'

His brown fingers stroked her forehead soothingly, brushing back her hair and making every touch a caress. Then with an arm around her waist he pulled her across his lap suddenly and held her close to the dark smoothness of his sun-warmed body. Held close in his arms, she looked up at him and stirred a little uneasily, her hands pressed to his chest. Heaven knew why she felt as she did, for she had seldom had doubts about Luigi before, but now, lying in his arms in this secret little cove, it seemed suddenly all wrong somehow, although she had no idea why it should.

'Luigi.'

Her doubt was expressed in her voice and she

would have pulled away from him, but his arms held her too tightly and his mouth was already on hers, more forceful than she had ever known it, and reminding her uneasily of the way Lucifer had kissed her. It was the thought of Lucifer that made her resist Luigi's arms, and she fought for breath when she managed to free her mouth at last and struggled to sit upright.

'*No, bella mia!*' Luigi was not easily shaken off and his arms were still tight around her, a bright glitter in his dark eyes that aroused unreasonable panic in her as she pushed at him, trying to get free. 'Rosalinda, *cara mia*——'

'Let me go, Luigi, please!'

She managed to break his hold at last and hastily scrambled to her feet, breathing hard and with a warm flush colouring her cheeks as she stood looking down at him, uncertain just why she was reacting the way she was. Luigi was puzzled, that was evident from the expression on his face, but he was annoyed too, for it was doubtful if he had ever suffered an outright rebuff before, and he did not relish the experience.

His dark eyes glittered and there was a tight, angry look about his mouth. Without a word he got to his feet, so giving himself the advantage of height, and for a second he stood facing her, his feet apart on the hot sand, his whole stance one of arrogant censure.

'Why do you treat me so?' he demanded, as if it was his right to know, and Rosalind shook her head.

'I'm sorry, Luigi,' she said, 'but——' Words failed her and she shrugged helplessly.

'You think to keep yourself for Lucifer?' he asked, in a harsh, unsteady voice, and she looked up quickly. 'You are a fool, *cara mia*, have I not told you so?'

Rosalind shook her head. Her eyes were bright with a curious blend of anger and hurt, and she looked at him steadily for a moment, then she turned her back on him and walked up the beach towards the path, unsure where she was going, only anxious to get away from him.

She was much too uncertain of her own feelings to try and explain them to Luigi, but she wished more fervently than ever that she had never allowed herself to be persuaded into coming. She had no clear idea of what she intended to do as she walked away from him, but it was only a matter of seconds before she heard him start after her.

'Rosalinda!' His voice was no longer arrogant but appealing and he was breathing rapidly as he ran to catch up with her, the words jerking out urgently as he ran. 'Rosalinda, *aspetti, per favore!*'

She did not stop but slowed down a little and he caught up with her, taking her arm and drawing her round to face him as he brought her to a halt. She could not imagine why she felt so tearful either, simply because he had made that malicious remark about Lucifer, or why there was a small chill feeling in her heart when she thought of how angry Lucifer was going to be.

There was contrition in Luigi's dark eyes when

she looked up at him, and the first hopeful signs of a smile on his mouth as he peered into her face. It was not easy to be angry with him and, if she was honest, it was not really fair either, for Luigi was simply being as he always was. Only her own confused feelings had made her react as she did.

She looked up at him and smiled a little ruefully. 'You're impossible,' she said huskily, but she let herself relax when he put his arms around her and pulled her close to his chest. She did not put up her hands or rest her head against him, but looked at the suddenly complacent smile on his mouth.

'*Carissima, amore mia!*' His arms tightened and his mouth sought hers, although she did nothing to encourage him, but simply allowed him, passively, to kiss her as if she had no feelings about it one way or the other. 'Rosalinda!' He brushed his mouth on hers, his voice reproachful. Then the arms about her tightened suddenly and he became tense, his eyes fixed on some point just beyond her. '*Dio mio!*' he murmured piously, and Rosalind turned her head swiftly to follow the direction of his gaze.

'Lucifer!'

She licked her lips and felt suddenly as if she had been trapped in a guilt-laden situation when she saw the tall, straight figure that came striding across the sandy beach towards them, for his frown was evident even from where she now stood. She pushed herself free of Luigi's arms and stepped back, watching that inexorable figure striding across the sand. Her heart was thudding relentlessly, although she had declared herself innocent of anything to do with Luigi's absence from that appointment he should have kept. Lucifer, she knew, would take quite a different view of her part in it, and she wished she could simply take to her heels and run.

He looked furiously angry and she hoped fervently that most of it was to be directed at Luigi, even though it was probably cowardly of her. The light grey suit he wore seemed to lend him additional height and his face looked much darker than usual, his black eyes narrowed and glittering like coals. He wasted no time in side issues, but spoke to Luigi in their own tongue, words so harsh that even the fluid Italian sounded hard and flat.

Rosalind was able to follow less than half of what he was saying and she felt suddenly very small and guilty as she stood there and tried not to listen while Luigi took the tirade, paling under his tan, but denying nothing. He looked at his watch and shrugged helplessly, murmuring excuses and offering momentary defiance which Lucifer dismissed with a contemptuous wave of his hand.

'Rosalinda.' Luigi looked past his brother and his eyes were both contrite and defiant, hating the situation more because he had no excuse and yet refused to admit he needed one. 'Lucifer has made excuses why I am not at this meeting,' he explained carefully. 'Another time has been arranged, but——' he shrugged, spreading his hands helplessly, 'I have one hour only to drive to Napoli and see this man. I cannot break this appointment again.'

'Oh, no, of course you can't!' she agreed hastily, and Luigi shrugged again helplessly.

'*Capisce?*'

'Yes, of course I understand,' she assured him, and looked at Lucifer from the corner of her eye. 'But will you have time to drive me back to the villa first?' she asked, and he shrugged uneasily.

It was Lucifer, however, who answered her. 'I am afraid he will not, Rosalinda,' he informed her shortly. 'I have persuaded Signor Candari to give Luigi another chance, but he does not have time to drive you back to the villa first.'

'Oh, I see, then——'

'You have little time, Luigi,' Lucifer interrupted her, turning back to his brother. 'Signor Candari is a patient man, but you have tried his patience beyond reason—he will not wait for you if you are not there to keep this appointment!'

'Then I will not trouble him!' Luigi retorted with a flash of impatience, and Lucifer's black eyes narrowed as he looked at him.

'When you are more certain that Mendori e Figli will never be yours,' he told him in a cold hard voice, 'then you may never see the *ufficio* again as long as you live, but until that is an established fact you will make an attempt to learn at least a little of the business! I refuse any longer to do it all alone, Luigi, *capisce?*'

Rosalind's head was spinning with speculation suddenly. He had told the Contessa that he had found someone he wanted to marry. She had been certain that was what he meant by that rather reticent statement at breakfast, and so had the Contessa. But if that was the case, why was he talking as if there was still a possibility that Luigi would be the eventual head of the firm?

Luigi glanced at her and his shoulders shrugged resignedly. '*Mi dispiace, cara*,' he said. 'Lucifer will——' He looked at his brother enquiringly. Lucifer said nothing but glanced at his wristwatch again, and once more Luigi shrugged. '*Addio, carissima*,' he said, and turned and walked off, leaving Rosalind alone on the little beach with Lucifer, who promised to be a far from genial substitute at the moment.

Neither of them moved or spoke for several moments, and it was almost as if he meant to be sure that Luigi was well away before he followed. Rosalind looked up at him, then hastily looked away again when she met the steady black gaze fixed on her speculatively. 'Will you drive me back?' she asked in a small voice, but he did not immediately answer and she curled her hands tightly. Whatever he had in mind she would refuse to accept all the blame for Luigi's negligence and she looked up again after a moment. Sticking out her chin, she met his eyes defiantly. 'Are you going to make me walk back?' she asked.

'Do you expect me to?' Lucifer retorted swiftly, and she shook her head.

'But you blame me for Luigi being here instead of keeping that appointment, don't you, Lucifer?'

The black eyes swept over her in a swift, bold

scrutiny that left her flushed and uneasy. 'No more than I would blame any other pretty face!' he informed her harshly, and Rosalind caught her breath. The jibe hurt far more than she was prepared to admit, but she could not let him know that.

'So you've sent Luigi off to his meeting and you intend to take it out on me!' she said, a bright, misty look in her eyes as she anticipated the worst.

He looked quite angry enough at the moment to send her packing, regardless of the Contessa's view, and she wondered how she would react if he did. For a second he looked at her steadily and she coped with the violent response her heart made to him. 'And what form do you anticipate your punishment will take, *signorina*?' he asked, with studied quietness.

Rosalind shook her head. Her every nerve responded to the force that emanated from him; that vigorous, ruthless aura of masculinity that seemed to reach out and envelop her as she stood facing him, so that she found it hard to think clearly. 'Are you going to dismiss me?' she suggested in a small, uncertain voice, and his black eyes gleamed.

'There is still the matter of your next month's salary,' he reminded her. 'Have you forgotten that?'

'No, of course not!'

She had, in fact, quite forgotten the money she had borrowed from him to pay for the blue silk dress, and she believed he really would make her work until she had paid it back. He had, she recalled, made some remark at the time about being sure she would not desert the Contessa in the meantime, and in some strange way it was a relief to know he could not simply dismiss her out of hand. Leaving the Villa Mimosa was the last thing she wanted to do, and she readily admitted it.

'Then you will work until you have repaid the loan,' he told her, and she glanced at him from the shadow of her long lashes—a tall, slightly menacing figure against the background of tree-covered cliff slopes and bright blue sky, so that she shivered involuntarily when he slid a large hand beneath her arm. 'I will drive you back to the villa,' he said. '*Vieni!*'

'I can——' She had been about to suggest that she could find her own way back, but she realised at once that the idea was quite ridiculous. They had driven some distance from Crisdorfi to reach the cove, and walking back was out of the question.

Lucifer was looking down at her enquiringly, almost as if he guessed what was in her mind. 'You prefer that I leave you here for Luigi to collect when he has finished with his meeting?' he asked, then shook his head without giving her an opportunity to answer. 'If you imagine I would leave you here, you do not know me very well, *piccola*!'

That 'little one' was somehow encouraging, but there was little else to encourage her about that strong, dark satyr's face. He accommodated his normal long stride to suit her, but she was still breathing heavily by the time they had crossed the sand and climbed more than half way up the steep path through the trees.

'How did you know where to find us?' she ventured breathlessly, as they neared the top.

'I know my brother very well,' he told her. 'Much better than you do, *mia ragazza*, and you told me yourself that he was bringing you here!'

She remembered then that she had indeed mentioned it to the Contessa while he was there. 'Then you couldn't really have been surprised to find us there!' she suggested, and Lucifer turned and looked down at her, his eyes holding hers for a moment until she hastily looked away.

'Would it surprise you to learn that I did *not* expect you to come with him when I had told you of that appointment?' he asked, and Rosalind did not answer for a moment. It was dismaying to realise that he had trusted her not to go with Luigi, perhaps depended on her refusal to ensure his brother's keeping the appointment, and she had let him down.

'I should say I'm sorry,' she suggested, and glanced up through her lashes. 'I—I simply let myself be persuaded, that's all.'

Lucifer turned his head and looked down at her for a second, and in some way she knew he was less angry than he had been. His eyes still glittered blackly, but there was a look about his mouth that suggested he saw a certain ironic amusement in the situation. 'Luigi finds the company of beautiful women quite irresistible,' he told her, and Rosalind's pulses skipped wildly at the implied compliment. 'It is unfortunate that he is unable to keep his priorities in order!'

'Unlike you!' Rosalind observed rashly. 'You'd never be guilty of putting pleasure before business, would you, Lucifer?'

The hand on her arm tightened its grip and she was swung round to face him so swiftly and suddenly that she gasped aloud and looked at him with wide, questioning eyes. The remembered strength of his arms bound her closely, making her aware of the unyielding hardness of his body, and she put up her hands instinctively, spreading them flat-palmed against his chest.

Under her fingers the steady, thudding beat of his heart pulsed away only slightly more rapidly than normal, and his black eyes, glittering darkly, filled her vision for a second before his mouth found hers. There was a fierce, passionate anger in his kiss that suggested a punishment rather than a caress, and she struggled, briefly, to escape, but one strong hand cradled her head and made escape impossible.

Instead, after only a few seconds, she yielded to the urgency of her own instincts, her body curving closer to the demanding arrogance of his, while her hands curled slowly on the broad span of his chest. The shirt he wore under his jacket was of fine white silk and there was a sensual smoothness in its touch with the heat of his body burning fiercely under her finger-tips.

She had expected it to go on for ever, instead he raised his head suddenly and, holding her at arm's length, he looked down at her. Flushed and dazed, she stared at him, her mouth still soft and warm from his kiss and her lips parted slightly as she recovered her breath.

'I was angry,' he said, his voice deep and only slightly unsteady. 'I should not have surprised you so—violently, Rosalinda.'

Rosalind, recovering her senses gradually, told herself that she would die of embarrassment if he apologised, and she turned from him quickly, her eyes brightly defensive, seeking to anticipate the reasons he might give for his action. 'You were simply proving that when it comes to it, you're quite capable of getting *your* priorities wrong too,' she said, and laughed a little breathlessly. 'Don't worry, Lucifer, there's no one here to see you this time!'

She was unsure of the precise meaning of the words he used, but there was no doubt that they were virulent and aptly expressed his feelings. His hand was once more under her arm and urging her along the steep cliff path, making less allowance now for her shorter step, so that she found it much harder going.

She was at a loss to understand her present mood as she struggled to keep pace with him, for she could have experienced any number of reactions in the circumstances. She had been kissed, forcefully and admittedly in anger, and then released as abruptly, and she could well have felt bewildered or even subdued. Instead there was a curious sense of intimacy about their present circumstance that she found curiously elating, and she said no more as they climbed towards the road.

There was no sign of Luigi's car, so presumably he had sped off to keep his appointment as Lucifer had said he should. Lucifer's car was parked under some trees and she realised that she had left her towel and swimsuit on the beach only when he was seeing her into the car. She hung back against the hand under her elbow and looked up at him warily.

'I've left my things on the beach,' she told him. 'I must go back for them!'

'Your handbag?' He looked down at her empty hands, but she was shaking her head.

'No, I hadn't a bag,' she said, 'just my swimsuit and a towel.'

'Ah!' He urged her into the car and closed the door on her, then strode round the car and got in beside her. 'I will not climb all that way back for a swimsuit,' he declared firmly. 'It is easily replaced!'

'Oh, but, Lucifer, it's a new one!' she protested as he started up the engine, and he turned and looked at her briefly, his eyes narrowed.

'Then send Luigi for it!' he told her shortly.

'Maybe you could add it to my bill,' she said pertly. 'Along with the dress I bought from Claudia Gerolamo!'

'And perhaps I will decide that you are too *impudente* to keep in my household, *poca strega*!' Lucifer declared, his black eyes gleaming.

Rosalind glanced at him as he put the big car into gear and they moved off swiftly along the motorway. His strong features looked dark and unrelenting, but there was something about his manner, about the look in those black eyes, that re-kindled that surge of elation. Little witch, he had called her—it could hardly be called an endearment, and yet in some strange way she believed he had meant it as one. The sea below the cliffs glittered and shone like blue glass in the bright sun, and she smiled to herself as she sat back. The matter of his chosen bride did not even enter her head.

Luigi, with his usual resilience, soon recovered from his encounter with Lucifer's anger, and Rosalind guessed that he would quite happily do the same thing again when the opportunity arose. It was easy to see why the Contessa was anxious to see Lucifer married and the firm safely in his hands—in Luigi's careless charge it would fare very much worse.

He walked with her in the garden after breakfast the following morning, his hand holding hers and his dark head bent over her attentively. He was very good for her ego, but lately she had begun to wish he was less extravagant in his admiration, although the Contessa was tolerant of his flirtations and saw them as a handsome couple.

'Today I have no stupid appointments with business men, *carissima*,' he told her. 'Where shall we go, huh?'

'I can't go anywhere,' Rosalind told him with a smile. 'I'm going to be very busy with the Contessa this morning, making out menus and answering letters. Besides, my morning off was yesterday.'

'And Lucifer ruined it!' Luigi declared. 'He

should let you have this morning in its place, *cara*; you should insist!'

Rosalind could well imagine herself insisting on having a free morning again today, and imagine what Lucifer's answer would be if she asked him too, and she smiled ruefully as she shook her head. 'I don't think so,' she said. 'Not after yesterday, Luigi. I'm not in a position to lay down the law, and anyway, I work for the Contessa, not Lucifer. She decides when I'm free!'

'Nonna decides only if Lucifer does not have other ideas,' Luigi informed her bluntly. 'He is *un tiranno*—a tyrant—my brother, no?'

'No,' Rosalind laughed, 'although he tries very hard to be one.'

Luigi's dark eyes reproached her. 'Always you defend him,' he said, making it obvious that she displeased him by doing so. 'Why is that, Rosa-linda?'

'Do I?' She did not look at him, and Luigi lifted her chin with one finger, dropping a light kiss on her mouth as he looked at her curiously.

'Always,' he insisted. 'I wish to know why, *cara mia*!'

In his own way he was as autocratic as Lucifer, she thought a little dazedly, and tried to find an answer that would not give him quite the wrong idea. 'Perhaps it's because I like him in spite of himself,' she confessed, and laughed uncertainly. 'Does that make sense?'

'No, *cara mia*, it does not!' Luigi declared firmly. 'No one can surely use such a word—like—

when talking of Lucifer, eh?'

It was true, of course, Rosalind realised. Like was not a word that Lucifer inspired, the feelings he aroused were much more fierce and intense. Stunned by the realisation, she faced the fact for the first time that Lucifer Mendori now played such an important part in her life that she could not imagine life without him.

'I like him,' she insisted, and hoped her voice did not betray anything more, for Luigi was looking at her curiously.

Then he bent his head and kissed her, laughing softly against her ear. 'It is as well you do not fall in love with him, *carissima*,' he told her, 'for Nonna has hinted to me that my brother has at last found a woman he wishes to marry.'

'Oh, but he isn't sure yet!' Rosalind denied hastily, and Luigi looked down at her with a frown. 'I—I was there when he told the Contessa about her yesterday morning,' she hastened to explain, and Luigi's eyes gleamed as he squeezed her hand encouragingly.

'Tell me, *bella mia*,' he urged, 'who is she? Do I know her? Do any of us know her, apart from Lucifer?'

'Luigi!' Freeing her hand from his, she walked a little way ahead of him and stood beside the pool, her heart fluttering anxiously. If the Contessa had told Luigi about her, Lucifer must be far more certain about his choice than he had sounded yesterday morning. 'I can't tell you anything about her,' she said when he came across to join her, 'and I wouldn't even if I could, Luigi. When Lucifer wants you to know he'll tell you himself!'

'But I am curious!' Luigi insisted, and she shrugged.

His curiosity was understandable and it could be no more avid than her own was, as she stood at the side of the pool gazing down at her own reflection in the water and wondering what kind of a woman Lucifer wanted to marry. Almost involuntarily she put a hand to her mouth and lightly touched her lips with a finger-tip, briefly reliving the heart-stopping excitement of Lucifer's kiss. Whoever the woman was she surely had no idea that he behaved so freely with his grandmother's secretary.

'Rosalinda!' Luigi's insistent voice spoke close to her ear and she brought herself hastily back to earth, turning to smile at him when he slid his hands around her waist and pulled her back until she was leaning against him. Bending his head, he kissed her neck lightly. 'Are you too not curious about Lucifer's *amante*?' he asked.

It was something more than curiosity she felt, Rosalind realised ruefully, she was actually jealous and she shook her head hastily to deny it to herself. 'I'm curious, I suppose,' she admitted, and Luigi laughed, kissing the lobe of her ear, his voice muffled by her long hair.

'Then ask questions, *mi amore*,' he said.

'Of Lucifer?' She turned and looked at him as if he had taken leave of his senses, breaking his hold on her and looking up at him for some time before she spoke again. 'You must be crazy to suggest such a thing,' she told him at last in a small voice. 'It doesn't concern anyone but Lucifer, and especially not me—I'm not even family!'

'Ah, but you can be very persuasive, *carissima*, I am sure,' he insisted with a laugh. 'Maybe Nonna knows something more than she will tell me—if so, *cara*, you could find out, woman to woman, *sì?*'

'No, Luigi!'

Laughing still, he reached out and pulled her into his arms again, nuzzling her neck with his face buried in her soft hair. '*Carissima,*' he said. 'I tease you, do I not?'

Rosalind said nothing. She moved out of his arms and turned back towards the house, feeling more uneasy than she ever had since she came to the villa. She could not even entertain the idea of discussing Lucifer's affairs with the Contessa, even if the old lady allowed it, and certainly not with the idea of passing any information she gathered on to Luigi.

She glanced at her watch as Luigi caught up with her, and he pulled a wry face. 'You are not late for your work, *cara*,' he told her. 'That would never do, would it?'

'I don't like to be late,' Rosalind said. 'The Contessa's very good to me and I wouldn't take advantage of it.'

He shrugged, walking beside her into the house. The Contessa was in the *salon* when they came in, sitting at her desk and sorting through letters that needed answering. She looked up and smiled and Luigi left Rosalind's side to go across to her, taking her gnarled hands gently in his and lightly kissing her fingers.

'Nonna,' he said, crouching beside her chair and wearing what Rosalind secretly called his soulful look. 'Are your *lettere* so very important this morning, *mia cara* Nonna?'

Rosalind had no difficulty in guessing what lay behind the question, and neither did the Contessa. She leaned over and kissed his forehead. 'You wish to take Rosalinda away from me, hmm?' she guessed, and glanced at Rosalind as if she had no doubt at all that she was also in favour of the idea. 'You would like to go, *bambina mia*?' she asked.

Rosalind was tempted, but she hated taking advantage of the old lady's goodness, so she shook her head rather half-heartedly. 'I can't, Contessa,' she said, 'we have an awful lot to do today and I had——'

'If you wish to go with Luigi then you shall,' the Contessa told her, making it a matter of fact. 'You surely would not rather stay and write *lettere*, would you?'

'But I had yesterday morning free,' Rosalind reminded her, making a stand against her conscience, and the Contessa pulled a wry face.

'And you did not have a very happy time, *cara*,' she said. 'It was bad of Luigi to go off with you when he should have kept the appointment in Napoli, but——' She shrugged in resignation, as if she was so used to her elder grandson's ways that she had long since become resigned to them. 'It was such a pity to spoil your swim and Lucifer was unkind to bring you home again.'

Again without stopping to think, Rosalind came to Lucifer's defence. 'Oh, but he was right to be angry about it,' she said. 'I shouldn't have encouraged Luigi to go to the cove; Lucifer had the embarrassment of explaining to Signor Candari and I could understand how he felt.'

'*Dio mio!*' Luigi breathed piously, looking across at her. 'Do you never tire of defending him, *bella mia?*' He looked up at his grandmother, his black brows arched meaningly and a hint of impatience in his dark eyes. 'Rosalinda has made herself Lucifer's—how do you say?—champion,' he told her, and the Contessa looked at her for a moment, her eyes steady and shrewd so that Rosalind hastily lowered her own gaze and wished with all her heart that she had been less impulsive.

'This is true, *bambina?*' she asked, and this time Rosalind leapt to her own defence.

'Not exactly, Contessa,' she denied in a small and rather husky voice. 'I—I simply don't think Lucifer's as black as Luigi likes to paint him, that's all. He *did* have the right to be angry yesterday and I can't very well blame him because he was.'

The old lady said nothing for several seconds but studied her with her shrewd dark eyes. Then she shook her head slowly, taking up the letters she had put down when Luigi came to her. 'You are right, *naturalmente,*' she said at last, 'but you will soon have no need to make yourself Lucifer's *campione.* He has, I think, no doubt in his own mind that he will ask this *misteriosa signorina* to marry him very soon now, and then he will no longer need your support, *piccola*.'

'Nonna!' Luigi looked at her with bright, curious eyes and it was obvious that he meant to find out more about his brother's mysterious love. 'Who is she, Nonna?' he asked eagerly. 'Do you know her name?'

The Contessa shook her head, '*No, caro mio*,' she said, a hand on his face and smiling faintly. 'But I know Luca, better than he knows—he has decided in his heart that he loves her, now he must decide with that *vero practico* head of his that she is worthy to be the Contessa Mendori! Then he will tell me!'

CHAPTER NINE

IT took Rosalind quite a long time to come to her decision, but eventually she was convinced that if Lucifer really did mean to marry his mysterious *signorina* then she had no other course open to her but to give up her job with the Contessa and return to England. The thought of staying on at the villa once he brought home his bride was unbearable, and became more so the more she thought about it.

She had realised the full depth of her feelings for him when she lay in bed last night, and the hopelessness of her situation had kept her awake until the small hours. She should have known, of course, that living and working under the same roof, day after day, with a man like Lucifer Mendori was almost bound to end with her falling in love with him. Only the presence of Luigi, charming and good-looking, had blinded her to the vulnerability of her position.

The Contessa, she thought, probably had some inkling of her feelings for Lucifer, hence that oblique warning concerning the role of his future wife as his champion, a chore that Luigi accused her of taking upon herself. It was doubtful if Luigi realised just how deep her concern was, but he had several times teased her about defending his brother in his absence, and warned her how foolish she would be to fall in love with him.

Tomorrow the first of the Contessa's visitors were due to arrive, although the succession of eligible young women that his grandmother had so hopefully arranged for him to choose from were now rather superfluous since he had made his own choice after all. It was when she thought about that that another idea came into her head, and she lay for a moment trying to decide whether or not Lucifer was devious enough to have thought of it too.

Judging by what she had heard via Luigi and the Contessa, he had made no mention of the woman he claimed to have fallen in love with until he learned of his grandmother's plans for him. Even now only he knew her name, if Luigi was to be believed, and she could not think why he was being so mysterious about her. Now, putting the two facts together, she wondered if he had merely invented that secret love of his simply as a defence against his grandmother's determined matchmaking.

Lying there thinking about it, she became more and more convinced she was right, and she almost laughed aloud as she gazed up at the gilded ceiling, dappled with morning shadows. If Lucifer was playing some devious game of his own and the secret lover did not exist, then—— Hastily she shook her head to clear it of any alternative ideas. There could be little question of her own position changing, although somehow it helped to believe he was still unattached and heart-free.

She was feeling much less unhappy as she bathed and dressed, and it startled her for a while to realise just how much he actually affected her life. Brushing her long fair hair, she looked at her reflection curiously and wondered if anyone else had noticed the different look in her eyes, or the soft flush that always seemed to colour her cheeks lately.

Putting down the brush at last, she smoothed her hands over the pale-blue dress she wore and smiled a little wryly. She had instinctively chosen blue because she had discovered, quite by accident, that it was Lucifer's favourite colour. Of course she was living in a fool's paradise even if Lucifer was deceiving his family with his story of being in love, but she could do nothing to stop the flush of hope it gave her.

She made her way down to the garden and found Lucifer and the Contessa already having breakfast.

There was no sign of Luigi, of course, it was much too soon for him to put in an appearance. The sunny garden with its shading trees was a familiar scene, one she had come to look forward to each morning. Lucifer was sitting there at the table with his grandmother, his dark head bent, his strong brown hands busy with the simple daily activity of breakfast, and her heart beat anxiously hard when she thought of it all coming to an end. If she did leave the villa and go home, then there could be no more breakfasts like this.

'*Buon giorno*, Rosalinda!' the Contessa called out to her as she came across the garden. She was evidently in exceptionally good spirits and Rosalind wondered if Lucifer had told her anything to make her so.

'*Buon giorno*, Contessa!' She looked across at Lucifer as she took her seat at the table. '*Buon giorno*, Lucifer.'

He answered with a smile that seemed to suggest he was about to make some remark but changed his mind at the last minute. '*Buon giorno*,' he murmured, and poured himself more coffee.

'That dress is *molto bella, cara*,' the Contessa told her with an approving smile. 'Is it new?'

Shaking her head, Rosalind smiled and she was unable to resist a meaningful glance in Lucifer's direction when she answered. 'Oh, no, Contessa,' she told her. 'I've had it for some time—I have to beware of buying too many new dresses. It must be the effect of the Italian sun, but I'm much too extravagant when I go out to buy a dress!'

There was a gleam of amusement in Lucifer's black eyes when he lifted his head, making it obvious that he knew what she referred to, and he cocked a dark brow at her. 'I hope you do not expect me to deny that,' he said, and Rosalind shook her head.

'I know you couldn't,' she told him. Every nerve in her body responded to the warmth of his smile, and she wished she was not so vulnerable. 'You know better than anyone where my extravagance can lead when I go shopping!' she told him, and the Contessa was looking from one to the other curiously.

'*Perchè dice ciò?*' she asked. 'Why do you say that, *cara?*'

'Do you not remember, Nonna?' Lucifer reminded her. 'Rosalinda had to borrow money to pay for the dress she had from Claudia Gerolamo.'

'The blue silk one—ah, *sì,* I remember!' The Contessa's dark eyes smiled at her. 'But you were wise to have that one, *bambina,* it suits you more than anything else that you have, I think. Does it not, Luca?'

'Of course the dress looks well, Nonna,' Lucifer agreed. 'Claudia Gerolamo does not make mistakes in such matters.'

But she does in the matter of taking Lucifer Mendori for granted, Rosalind thought wildly, and hastily recalled the memory of the vase that had come hurtling after them as they left Claudia Gerolamo's *salon* in Naples. Only a man like Lucifer could arouse such passions of anger and jealousy, and it still gave her a strange sense of satisfaction to realise that she had been the cause of the red-haired woman's jealousy. That and Lucifer's rather offhand parting from her had been the reason they left so spectacularly.

Hastily bringing herself back to earth, she smiled at the Contessa. 'That's the most expensive dress I've ever owned in my life,' she confessed, 'and I really shouldn't have had it. If Lucifer *hadn't* let me borrow from my next pay cheque I don't know what I'd have done!'

'But did you ever doubt that I would help you?' Lucifer asked, fixing her with his black eyes steadily. 'Surely not, *piccola!*'

Something in his voice, in that softly spoken 'little one', made the Contessa look at him sharply, Rosalind thought, and brought a flush of colour to her own cheeks. If only she had more control over her reactions to him! she thought desperately. The Contessa was bound to have noticed her blush and put her own interpretation on it.

'I could only hope you'd come to my rescue,' Rosalind said in a small and slightly breathless voice. She reached for the coffee pot and filled her cup. 'Anyway, I was very grateful, even if I do owe you slave time for it!'

He looked at her curiously, his eyes narrowed and glittering with what she took to be laughter. 'Slave time?' he queried. 'What *do* you mean, Rosalinda?'

Rosalind glanced uneasily from one to the other before she answered. She had thought it a simple enough statement, but apparently neither of them had heard it before and she felt suddenly as if she had said something far more provocative than she had intended. She shrugged, making light of it, and smiled at Lucifer.

'It means that I owe you time in working hours for the money I borrowed,' she explained. 'It's an old expression.'

'Ah!' He laughed and shook his head slowly. 'In return for learning Italian you teach me colloquial English!' He held her gaze steadily for a moment and smiled. 'Tomorrow you have your next pay cheque,' he reminded her. 'You will no longer owe me slave time, *piccola*—we shall no longer be sure of you staying with us, hmm?'

It was a suggestion much too close to her own recent thoughts and she looked at him with wide, startled eyes for a moment before she realised that his choice of words was pure coincidence. 'I—I haven't stayed simply because I owed you time,' she said, her voice not quite steady. 'But perhaps—in a little while——' She struggled with an explanation that was going to sound very feeble and unconvincing unless she gave it a great deal more thought, and she was grateful when the Contessa came to her rescue.

'*Naturalmente* Rosalinda will not be leaving me, *caro*,' she informed her grandson confidently. 'There is much to do in the coming weeks and I cannot manage without her—is that not so, Rosalinda?'

There was nothing to do but agree, Rosalind

thought, so she nodded, glancing briefly at Lucifer before she did so. 'I won't desert you, Contessa,' she promised. 'Not while you need me.'

'Nor ever!' the Contessa decreed expansively. 'You are grown close to me, *bambina mia*, and I would miss you. Very soon now our visitors will be here and the house will be filled—then I will surely need you!'

'Filled with your friends and their charming daughters, Nonna?' Lucifer suggested, and his black eyes glittered as he gently teased the old lady for her plotting on his behalf.

The Contessa looked at him shrewdly for a moment, then leaned across and touched his hand lightly with her fingertips. 'Will you not invite your *signorina* to join us also, *caro*?' she suggested. 'I would so much like to meet her, and it would be an excellent time to announce *il fidanzamento*.'

Lucifer said nothing for a moment, but Rosalind's heart was beating urgently and anxiously as she waited to hear his reply. Suggesting that an engagement should be announced was pushing him into a corner, she realised.

If the woman did not exist, as she half suspected then he would have to make some excuse, but the Contessa would not be easily put off, and she watched him while he broke a crisp new brioche and spread it lavishly with butter. Outwardly he appeared calm and unconcerned, but Rosalind would have given much to know what was going on in his mind.

'I will see what can be done, Nonna,' he told her

after a while. 'It is a little soon for such firm plans.'

The Contessa frowned, suspicious at last, and Rosalind felt uneasily superfluous. 'Luca——' The old lady hesitated, unwilling to believe her own suspicions. 'Can you mean that you have not yet spoken to the *signorina*?' she asked.

Lucifer's black eyes glanced briefly at Rosalind, and once more, as she had that morning at breakfast when the matter was first mentioned, she got the feeling that he felt the subject too personal to be discussed in front of her. Putting down her coffee cup, a bright flush on her cheeks, she looked across at the Contessa.

'I'll leave you, Contessa,' she said. 'You have things to talk about that—that don't really concern me, and Lucifer——'

'There is no need for you to go, *piccola*,' Lucifer interrupted. 'Announcing an engagement is premature at this point, since I have not yet spoken to the *signorina* herself of the matter. There is nothing more to discuss!'

For a moment Rosalind hesitated. Maybe he was delaying the moment when he had to tell the Contessa that his secret lover did not exist, but somehow she felt convinced now that she did exist, and her heart thudded sickeningly hard in her breast. Making up her mind at last, she got to her feet. She had had no more than a cup of coffee, but she had no appetite for breakfast and she had her own future to think over seriously.

'I don't feel like breakfast,' she told him, managing a smile, even though it did not reach her eyes.

'If you'll excuse me, I have one or two things to do before I start work.'

'*Naturalmente!*' The Contessa's dark eyes were watching her curiously as she turned to go. 'You are not unwell, are you, *cara*?' she asked, and Rosalind shook her head.

'Oh, no, Contessa, I'm perfectly well, thank you!'

They watched her go, she knew, she could feel their eyes follow her and sense the heavy silence that disguised their curiosity, and there was nothing she could do about the tears that trembled on her lashes. She had been almost certain that Lucifer had invented his mystery lady, now she was certain he hadn't, and the certainty made her feel curiously numb.

Luigi had come to look upon it almost as his right to walk with her in the garden after dinner, and she had to admit that she had on the whole enjoyed his company. This evening, however, she felt like being on her own and she hoped to slip out of the house without his following her.

She was part way across the hall when Adolfo appeared and looked at her with his inscrutable black eyes, inclining his head in a brief bow. Even that she viewed with doubt, for Adolfo never failed to make her feel uneasy. 'The *signorina* walks alone?' he enquired, polite as usual and yet managing to convey a certain insolence that brought a flush to her cheeks.

'Not very far,' she said, trying not to sound too

short with him, for she felt rather guilty about not liking him when Lucifer set such store by him. 'Just down the hill.'

'*Signorina!*' Once more that small polite bob conveyed both respect and familiarity, and he stood back while she walked past him to the door.

It would not really have mattered if she had told Adolfo where she intended going, for he had little love for Luigi and would be very unlikely to pass the information on to him. His attachment to Lucifer was unshakable, so the Contessa had told her, but no one else was so high in his esteem.

Shrugging off the enigma that was Adolfo, she made her way down the steep narrow road towards the bay of Crisdorfi. It had once been a familiar walk during her first couple of weeks there, but since the advent of Luigi she had done much less walking and consequently had less time to appreciate the more tranquil aspects of the village.

The narrow road wound like a dusty snake down the cliff face, giving a different view at every turn, and all of them breathtaking, especially at this time of the day. The ocean appeared to be a much deeper blue in the evening light, glowing with a dull gold from the dying sun. The same colour that gave the white houses a more mellow look and turned the sky into an artist's palette.

The cool of evening stirred among the scented trees and wafted the familiar perfume of the lemons about her as she walked down the twisty road towards the quay. She missed a great deal by riding around in Luigi's car and she was only now beginning to realise it.

The first boats were already setting out from the harbour for the evening's fishing, leaving little ruffles of white lace in their wake on the blue water. Stout little boats with their red sails drawn against the evening sky, and Rosalind smiled as she watched them. She had loved being in Crisdorfi and she doubted if she would ever find anywhere else as idyllic, no matter where she went after this. It came as a shock to her a few seconds later to re-alise that she was already thinking of her stay in the past tense.

She had put on a deep blue dress, softly cut to flatter her shape, although she told herself that she could not hope that Lucifer would notice what she wore when he had his *signorina* in mind. However she was going to stay and cope with the Contessa's guests if Lucifer's fiancée was among them, she had no idea, but she had given her word to stay now and she would find it hard to go back on it.

Just before she reached the quay, she paused and leaned on the stone wall that curved with the winding road, looking down at the peaceful tran-quillity of Crisdorfi in the lull of evening. An occasional murmur of voices reached her, a child crying, a woman calling; indefinite, comfortable sounds that somehow made her feel more unhappy than ever.

'Rosalinda!'

She did not turn from her view of the sea, but stayed where she was, her heart fluttering uneasily when she recognised Luigi's voice behind her. The wonder was that he had followed her on foot, it would have been more in keeping with his character if he had driven his car, ready to whisk her off somewhere—and evidently Adolfo was less reliable than she had thought.

He arrived in a flurry of excitement, puzzled by her departure and probably a little annoyed too because she had said nothing to him about coming out. A hand, confident and possessive, slid about her slim waist and his face was pressed to hers as he kissed her cheek.

'How did you know where to find me?' she asked without turning her head, and he laughed softly.

'I saw you from my window, *carissima*,' he told her. 'You could have gone nowhere else but to the bay, taking this road.'

Rosalind pushed his arms from her waist and moved away from him, sensing his frown as she did so. 'I came out because I wanted to be alone,' she told him. 'I didn't want you—anyone to follow me, Luigi, and I'm sorry you did.'

He said nothing for a moment, but she knew he was watching her, leaning on the stone wall only a foot or so away, his dark, handsome head outlined against the darkening sky over the bay. 'Not even Lucifer?' he asked after a few moments, and Rosalind turned swiftly, her eyes wide and hurt, so that he hastily avoided looking at her and instead turned to look down at the scene she had been watching.

'I *would* like to be alone for a bit, Luigi,' she said in a small and rather unsteady voice, and he nodded.

'*Mi dispiace*, Rosalinda,' he said. 'I am sorry.'

She still managed to contain the tears that threatened, but it was difficult and she did not know how much longer she could manage. 'Why should you be sorry?' she asked, shaking her head. 'You've done nothing to apologise for, Luigi, and I'm sorry I gave the impression.'

Again he was silent for several seconds, then he shook his head, his hands thrust into the front pockets of his trousers, not looking at her as he spoke. 'I will go away and leave you, *carissima*,' he told her. 'But if you need——'

'A shoulder to cry on,' Rosalind interrupted hastily, 'I'll call on you, Luigi, thank you.'

He nodded and for a moment looked as if he might say something else, then he shrugged his shoulders in a gesture that expressed his resignation in the face of insurmountable odds, and kissed her lightly on her cheek. '*Ciao, cara mia*,' he said softly, and turned to walk back up the hill.

For a while Rosalind toyed with the idea of visiting Signora Vincente, for she needed someone to talk to, but the memory of the Signora's taste for gossip made her a bad choice of confidante. Instead she walked right down to the quay where the rest of the fishing fleet were setting out after anchovy in the deepening dusk, finding a curious sense of comfort in their departure.

She sat on the quay for a while, watching the sun set and the lights come on in the villas scattered down the cliff side, like fireflies suspended in the dusk. It was almost dark when she stood up at last and turned to walk back, and the sound of a car engine shattered the evening still as it came down the cliff road.

It turned on the narrow quay just before she got that far and she recognised Lucifer's sleek dark Lancia only when she walked alongside and Lucifer got out. She stopped short, her heart thudding wildly with the sudden erratic drawing of her breath. Striding round the car, he came and stood immediately in front of her, looking down at her in the dying light and saying nothing.

'Lucifer?' Her voice trembled and there was nothing she could do to stop it as she gazed up at the dark, satyr's face, the features more deeply graven than ever and the black eyes glowing like coals. 'Why are you here?' she asked, and briefly white teeth slashed a smile across the shadowed features.

'Because when I asked Teresa to find you for me you were not there,' he said, and the deep softness of his voice shivered along her spine. He slid a hand under her arm, his fingers firm and persuasive on her soft skin. 'I have to speak to you, *piccola*,' he told her. 'Come with me, *per favore.*'

'Where—where to?' It did not matter in the least where he wanted to take her, but she needed a moment to think, to put her chaotic thoughts in order.

He was smiling again, and the arm he held was squeezed gently against his side, the warmth of his body impressed on her cool skin. 'Somewhere that Luigi will not find us,' he said, and laughed softly as if something pleased him suddenly. 'He came back alone, Rosalinda. Did you send him away?'

She could not understand him at all, not his desire to speak to her alone, nor his apparent pleasure because she had sent Luigi away so that she could be alone. 'I wanted to be on my own,' she said in a small unsteady voice. 'I've a lot to think about.'

'*Sì, cara mia,* you have,' he agreed, and urged her towards the car. 'We will drive to where it is quiet and I will help you to decide, *sì*?'

He saw her into the car and slid into the seat beside her, starting the engine without another word, but turning briefly to smile at her as they drove off. Her mind was in complete chaos and nothing made sense any more, but she could think of nowhere she would rather be than driving through a moonlit Italian night with Lucifer— wherever they were going.

They drove further than Rosalind expected, not towards Naples but along the motorway towards the less populated areas. The moon was high by the time they turned into a small tree-shaded spot beside the road, a fat silver moon that shed flashes of glittering light over the dark surface of the sea like sequins on dark silk, and the breathtaking scent of lemons still filled the air from the groves on the other side of the road.

Lucifer opened the door for her and extended a hand to help her, saying nothing still but smiling when she glanced up at him. It was like being on top of the world and she walked with him to the edge of the steep incline, looking down at the tops of trees and the glittering sea beyond.

He let her gaze at it for several seconds, then slowly turned her to face him, his hands strong and persuasive, their touch stirring her heart beat to a wild, breathtaking beat that made her head spin. 'Rosalinda!' There was no resisting that deep, persuasive voice nor the glow in his black eyes as they looked down at her. 'You know that I have promised to bring my *amante* to meet the Contessa?' he asked, and Rosalind drew a sharp breath as she looked up at him, her eyes suddenly wide and wary.

'She does exist?' she whispered faintly, and he frowned at her for a moment curiously.

'*Naturalmente, diletta mia*,' he said. 'Why should you doubt it?'

'I thought you might have invented her,' she whispered breathlessly. 'To—because the Contessa has such plans to find you a wife and you—you don't like being forced into anything. I thought you'd made her up just to play for time.'

'Play for time!' He repeated the unfamiliar phrase musingly, and shrugged his broad shoulders as he looked down at her. 'I was, as you say, playing for time, *piccola*, because I was being put in a position where I had to act much more quickly than I wished on a matter that is very important to me.

Not only to me, but to the woman I hope to make my wife—I would like to have given her more time, let her grow more—accustomed to me, but Nonna—how is it you say?—forced my hand!'

'I see.' She saw very little at all, in fact, but her head was filled with so many questions, so many things she did not pretend to understand that she could not think at all clearly about anything. 'I—I don't quite see why you wanted to speak to me about it,' she ventured after a moment, and Lucifer looked down at her steadily.

'Rosalinda,' he said softly, 'I would like to have given you more time, but I have given my word to the Contessa that I will bring to her the woman I love by tomorrow night, before her friends arrive. Will you marry me, Rosalinda?'

Too stunned to answer him, Rosalind stared at him for several seconds, her eyes dark and luminous in the moonlight, her mouth tremulous and her lips parted in surprise. It was not what she had expected to hear from him and she could not bring her chaotic reactions under control sufficiently to grasp the full meaning of what he said.

'Rosalinda?' His hands were strong and urgent in their pressure, gripping her as if in desperation, and the black eyes glowed in the uncertain light. 'I love you, *piccola*,' he told her softly. 'Will you not say you will marry me?'

'Oh, Lucifer!' It was all she could manage at the moment and her voice shivered, almost soundless, on the cool night breeze.

The hands on her arms tightened their hold and

Rosalind's heart felt as if it would tear itself from her body if she did not yield to its clamour. 'I have loved you long enough to be sure of my love,' Lucifer said in that deep persuasive voice she loved so much. 'I had to be sure, you see, *diletta*, very sure! Now I must be sure that you love me!'

'Lucifer!' She whispered his name, scarcely daring to believe she was actually hearing him say that he loved her. That he was standing there close to her with his dark, arrogant head bent over her and his black eyes looking down at her with a deep, unfathomable glow in their darkness. 'I—I can't believe you really mean it,' she whispered, and put her arms around him suddenly, burying her face against his chest. 'I can't believe it! I loved you so much, and——'

'*Amare mia!*' His arms were around her, crushing her to him until she bowed her own slim body to his unyielding strength. His face was buried in her long hair and his voice muffled as he murmured endearments, kissing her lightly between each one until, breathless, she raised her face and looked up at him, her eyes huge and shining in the soft light.

'I cried,' she said huskily. 'I cried because I thought you loved someone else, I didn't know it was—— Oh, darling Lucifer, I still can't believe it's me!'

Lucifer held her close against him, looking down at her face, his black eyes moving slowly over each feature as if he would never tire of its familiarity. 'You are so young, *carissima*,' he said. 'I was afraid to be in too much hurry for fear I made you wary of me. Also you seemed to be so—attached to Luigi that sometimes I almost hated him for being so close to you!'

'Luigi was never really close to me,' she denied, and tiptoed to brush her mouth lightly against his. 'You've made me so unhappy these past few days,' she whispered, 'I could almost have hated *you*!'

'*Amare mia!*' His mouth sought hers, firm and demanding, his arms binding her close to the strong, sensual vigour of his body. Strong gentle hands pushed the blue dress from her shoulder and he pressed his mouth to her soft, scented skin, kissing her neck and the smooth, vulnerable warmth of her throat. '*Diletta mia*,' he murmured. 'My beloved, will you not say that you will marry me?'

Rosalind leaned back in his arms, her own twined about his neck, so close she could feel the throbbing urgency of his heart beat with her own. '*Sì, amore mio*,' she said softly. 'I'll marry you.' The scent of lemons surrounded them, sweet on the cool night air, and she lifted her mouth to him once more.

romance is beautiful!

and Harlequin Reader Service is your passport to the Heart of Harlequin

Harlequin is the world's leading publisher of romantic fiction novels. If you enjoy the mystery and adventure of romance, then you will want to keep up to date on all of our new monthly releases—eight brand new Romances and four Harlequin Presents.

If you are interested in catching up on exciting and valuable back issues, Harlequin Reader Service offers a wide choice of best-selling novels reissued for your reading enjoyment.

If you want a truly jumbo read and a money-saving value, the Harlequin Omnibus offers three intriguing novels under one cover by one of your favorite authors.

To find out more about Harlequin, the following information will be your passport to the Heart of Harlequin.

collection editions

**Rare Vintage Romance
From Harlequin**

The Harlequin Collection editions have been chosen
from our 400 through 899 series, and comprise some of
our earliest and most sought-after titles. Most of the
novels in this series have not been available since the
original publication and are available now in beautifully
redesigned covers.

When complete, these unique books will comprise the
finest collection of vintage romance novels available.
You will treasure reading and owning this delightful
library of beautiful love stories for many years to come.

For further information, turn to the back of this book and
return the INFORMATION PLEASE coupon.

the omnibus

A Great Idea! Three great romances by the same author, in one deluxe paperback volume.

A Great Value! Almost 600 pages of pure entertainment for only $1.95 per volume.

Essie Summers

Bride in Flight (#933)
...begins on the eve of Kirsty's wedding with the strange phone call that changed her life. Blindly, instinctively Kirsty ran — but even New Zealand wasn't far enough to avoid the complications that followed!

Postscript to Yesterday (#1119)
...Nicola was dirty, exasperated and a little bit frightened. She was in no shape after her amateur mechanics on the car to meet any man, let alone Forbes Westerfield. He was the man who had told her not to come.

Meet on My Ground (#1326)
...is the story of two people in love, separated by pride. Alastair Campbell had money and position — Sarah Macdonald was a girl with pride. But pride was no comfort to her at all after she'd let Alastair go!

Jean S. MacLeod

The Wolf of Heimra (#990)
...Fenella knew that in spite of her love for the island, she had no claim on Heimra yet — until an heir was born. These MacKails were so sure of themselves; they expected everything to come their way.

Summer Island (#1314)
...Cathie's return to Loch Arden was traumatic. She knew she was clinging to the past, refusing to let it go. But change was something you thought of happening in other places — never in your own beloved glen.

Slave of the Wind (#1339)
...Lesley's pleasure on homecoming and meeting the handsome stranger quickly changed to dismay when she discovered that he was Maxwell Croy — the man whose family once owned her home. And Maxwell was determined to get it back again.

Susan Barrie

Marry a Stranger (#1034)
... if she lived to be a hundred, Stacey knew she'd never be more violently in love than she was at this moment. But Edouard had told her bluntly that he would never fall in love with her!

Rose in the Bud (#1168)
... One thing Cathleen learned in Venice: It was highly important to be cautious when a man was a stranger and inhabited a world unfamiliar to her. The more charm he possessed, the more wary she should be!

The Marriage Wheel (#1311)
... Admittedly the job was unusual — lady chauffeur to Humphrey Lestrode; and admittedly Humphrey was high-handed and arrogant. Nevertheless Frederica was enjoying her work at Farthing Hall. Then along came her mother and beautiful sister, Rosaleen, to upset everything.

Violet Winspear

Beloved Tyrant (#1032)
... Monterey was a beautiful place to recuperate. Lyn's job was interesting. Everything, in fact, would have been perfect, Lyn Gilmore thought, if it hadn't been for the hateful Rick Corderas. He made her feel alive again!

Court of the Veils (#1267)
... In the lush plantation on the edge of the Sahara, Roslyn Brant tried very hard to remember her fiancé and her past. But the bitter, disillusioned Duane Hunter refused to believe that she ever was engaged to his cousin, Armand.

Palace of the Peacocks (#1318)
... Suddenly the island, this exotic place that so recently had given her sanctuary, seemed an unlucky place rather than a magical one. She must get away from the cold palace and its ghost — and especially from Ryk van Helden.

Isobel Chace

The Saffron Sky (#1250)
... set in a tiny village skirting the exotic Bangkok, Siam, the small, nervous Myfanwy Jones realizes her most cherished dream, adventure and romance in a far-off land. Two handsome men determine to marry her, but both have the same mysterious reason....

A Handful of Silver (#1306)
... in exciting Rio de Janeiro, city of endless beaches and skyscraper hotels, a battle of wits is waged between Madelaine Delahaye, Pilar Fernandez, the jealous fiancée of her childhood friend, and her handsome, treacherous cousin — Luis da Maestro....

The Damask Rose (#1334)
... Vicki Tremaine flies to the heady atmosphere of Damascus to meet Adam Templeton, fiancé of the rebellious Miriam. But alas, as time passes, Vicki only becomes more attracted to this young Englishman with the steel-like personality....

Jane Arbor

A Girl Named Smith (#1000)
...Mary Smith, a girl with a most uninspired name, a mouselike
personality and a decidedly unglamorous appearance. That was how
Mary saw herself. If this description had fitted, it would have been a great
pleasure to the scheming Leonie Crispin and could have avoided a
great deal of misunderstanding between Mary, Leonie and the
handsomely attractive Clive Derwent....

Kingfisher Tide (#950)
...Rose Drake was about to realize her most cherished dream — to
return to the small village of Maurinaire, France. The idea of managing
her aunt's boutique shop produced grand illusions for Rose, but from the
very day of her arrival, they were turned to dismay. The man responsible
was the town's chief landowner and seigneur, a tyrant — living back in
the days of feudalism....

The Cypress Garden (#1336)
...at the Villa Fontana in the Albano Hills in Italy, the young, pretty
Alessandra Rhode is subjected to a cruel deception that creates
enormous complications in her life. The two handsome brothers who
participate pay dearly for their deceit — particularly, the one who
falls in love....

Anne Weale

The Sea Waif (#1123)
...it couldn't be, could it? Sara Winchester, the beautiful and talented
singer, stood motionless gazing at the painting in the gallery window. As
she tried to focus through her tears, her thoughts went racing back to her
sixteenth birthday, almost six years ago, and the first time she had set
eyes on the sleek black-hulled sloop *Sea Wolf* and its owner, Jonathon
"Joe" Logan....

The Feast of Sara (#1007)
...as Joceline read and re-read the almost desperate letter just received
from cousin Camilla in France, pleading with Joceline to come and be
with her, she sensed that something was terribly wrong. Immediately,
she prepared to leave for France, filled with misgivings; afraid of
learning the reason for her cousin's frantic plea....

Doctor In Malaya (#914)
...Andrea Fleming desperately wanted to accompany the film crew on
the expedition, but Doctor James Ferguson was adamantly opposed,
stating that if she went along, he would refuse to guide them. But
Guy Ramsey had other ideas, and cunningly devised a scheme
whereby Andrea would join them — in a manner the Doctor could do
nothing about....

information please

**All the Exciting News from
Under the Harlequin Sun**

It costs you nothing to receive our news bulletins and intriguing brochures. From our brand new releases to our money-saving 3-in-1 omnibus and valuable best-selling back titles, our information package is sure to be a hit. Don't miss out on any of the exciting details. Send for your Harlequin INFORMATION PLEASE package today.

| MAIL COUPON TO | Harlequin Reader Service, M.P.O. Box 707, Niagara Falls, New York 14302. |

| Canadian SEND Residents TO: | Harlequin Reader Service, Stratford, Ont. N5A 6W4 |

Please send me the free Harlequin Information Package

Name _____

Address _____

City _____

State/Prov. _____

Zip/Postal Code _____